I0542047

# WORTH THE WAIT

# DESTINY MOON

Worth the Wait
ISBN # 978-1-78430-519-2
©Copyright Destiny Moon 2015
Cover Art by Posh Gosh ©Copyright March 2015
Interior text design by Claire Siemaszkiewicz
Totally Bound Publishing

# WORTH THE WAIT

# Dedication

For B.

# Prologue

I'm not crazy, I swear. Okay, okay, maybe I'm a little bit nuts. I'm basically in love with my boss, Jerome, and that is a recipe for craziness. Other than that, though, I'm totally normal.

Somehow I found myself in Jerome's neighborhood, right at the corner in front of his building, like some sort of deranged stalker. Stupidly — maybe even moronically — I had to walk by to see if his light was on.

It was. He was home. I couldn't tell who was over but there was definitely someone with him. He lived on the top floor of a three-story walk-up and I could tell they had a movie on or something because of the flickering from the TV. My heart sank. Insta-jealous.

I headed in the direction of home, in the rain, feeling like a total loser, with my aching heart and obsessive mind punishing me. Who was over? Why did he have to be so hard to read?

There is really nothing worse than an office crush, especially on the world's sexiest boss. Every other guy at the office was easy to read — too easy, most of them—but Jerome was an Escher painting. Sometimes I thought I was looking at something beautiful albeit challenging to decode, but the longer I looked, the more I realized that it was one big mystery after another and it could never be solved. He was infuriating. But so was I, because I couldn't stop looking.

Last week it was the way he'd brought a box of ice cream sandwiches back to the office after his coffee break. It had been a sunny, cloud-free afternoon, the kind that made corporate employees stare out of the window and question their life choices. Morale was low. In walked Jerome with a bit of summer fun as we headed into fall. He was so thoughtful. He didn't have to do that. Certainly none of the other department heads did stuff like that. It wasn't expected and I doubted that he could submit the receipt as petty cash, meaning that he'd paid for them himself. Of course, it wasn't the money, but the thought.

Naturally, after he'd given me my ice cream sandwich I'd spent the rest of the afternoon swooning and lost all ability to concentrate. He brings that out in me. I can't focus around him. Not that I blame him. I'm pretty sure every woman at the office feels this way, not just me. It's not his fault he's been gifted with animal magnetism. It's just irritating.

What's worse, he's got the power to lure a girl in, but then he pushes her away again. At least that's my impression and I've been paying pretty close attention for the past year or so. He'll smile at a waitress when we're out for a corporate function, and she'll flirt with him then he'll totally lock her out. It's like he can't help but be this sexy guy that everyone wants, but he's not actually available. He's the ungettable get.

I wanted to know who he was spending time with. My mind raced as I speed-walked through the congested city streets, urging myself to mind my own business and not overthink every little detail of my boss's actions.

I stopped in at the greengrocer's to get a few bananas and a basket of blueberries for my morning smoothie. A guy came up to me as I was choosing bananas.

"Excuse me," he said, "do you know how to pick out grapefruit?"

He was playing helpless. Classic. I'd heard this pick-up line in action before. I rolled my eyes. *Men are pathetic.*

"Here," I said, tossing a few citrus fruits into his basket.

"I thought I should tell you you're beautiful." He smiled at me.

"Do I look drunk to you?" I sneered. I realized how rude I'd sounded, so I added, "Sorry. I hate men right now and I just want to go home."

He backed away from me like I was a bomb about to go off. Men could be such drama queens. What had he been thinking, anyway? He'd compliment me and I'd just go home with him?

Of course the more I thought of it, the more I realized that this was precisely the kind of guy I used to go home with, before Jerome came into my world. Men were easy then. They showed signs of interest and if I was horny or drunk, I went with them. We had our little roll in the hay and that was that. Easy. Guys like Mr. Produce Pick-Up weren't the problem. It was Jerome. He was the problem. He had single-handedly ruined my relationship with men as a species.

At home, I took a bath to drown out the frustrations of the day. If I was doomed to be fantasizing again, at least I had sex toys and plenty of them.

Time for a gin martini and that scene from Sarah Polley's movie, *Take This Waltz*. Thank God I had invested in that DVD. Threesomes seem like a really fun idea. Too bad they involve real people. Sometimes real people suck.

# Chapter One

Jerome was insufferable today. He looked way too good in his suit, like a pastry that tormented you by calling your name all the way from the bakery. In his navy blue and gray pinstripes with a crisp purple shirt underneath, he looked like he'd stepped out of the pages of *GQ*. He even had on those sexy glasses. He either had a gay best friend or a savvy girlfriend who dressed him. He was like no other straight guy I'd ever met... And I'd met a lot. I knew men. And Jerome was in a category all on his own.

At four, he sidled up to my desk and asked me if I had a moment.

For him? Of course!

"I'd like your analysis report of the Murdoch file before you leave," he said. He knew I couldn't do it in an hour.

"Okay," I responded.

That saucy flirt had basically invited me to stay late with him. Classic. So I did what any hot-blooded girl with an out-of-control libido would do. I took a quick coffee break, went down to the mall below our office tower and bought myself some lucky panties. *You just never know.* I had to cling to the hope that he had ulterior motives.

* * * *

At six o'clock, he asked what I wanted for dinner. On him, he said, since he was forcing me to work late. I told him we should have sushi. That was better than something greasy, I figured. Keep it light. After all, who knew what we'd get up to later?

I figured that tonight was the night he was going to tell me he felt the same way about me that I did about him. I pictured him coming over to my desk, telling me he couldn't stand how sexy I was, that I was a terrible distraction for him. I would be so glad I had gone to L'Atmosphere to pick up a frilly little number. It occurred to me that I should really keep a pair at work for just such an emergency.

By quarter after six, there was no one left but us. The lights in the other areas were all turned off for the evening. It was much dimmer in here than usual. Mood lighting. He was going to find a way to finally turn business into pleasure and all I had to do was bide my time until he came over, swept everything off my desk and took me in a passionate embrace.

* * * *

No such luck. By the time I got home, I was shaking my head. *That guy! Seriously. Nothing. Nada.* He'd got me to stay late to…*work?* Who did that? When dinner had arrived, I'd suggested that we eat together and he'd said he'd rather just keep on working and asked me if I wouldn't rather eat at my desk and get home at a decent hour. Well, I'd got home later than usual, twenty bucks poorer because of my panty-splurge.

He really had some nerve. I would have loved to tell him off, tell him that no other guy would ever treat me that way. But I guessed that was just it. He was not like other guys.

I called Claudia. At least she'd understand.

"Men suck," I huffed.

"Yeah," she said. "They can be slobs. Pete's laundry is spread all over again and I can't stand it. He treats our place like a hotel."

That was true. I wanted to tell her I thought she was settling, but I couldn't do it. It was a bigger discussion and it'd have to wait. She provided more proof that men are hate-worthy and that shacking up with one just made him lazy and gross. I told her about Jerome's infuriating behavior.

"Maybe he's hiding something," Claudia suggested.

"He is, right?" Her theory felt accurate to me. "But what?"

I ran my gay theory by her, but she didn't think that was it. "Nobody hides that anymore. There's no reason to."

"You're right, but you should see how he dresses. He's definitely metrosexual. I mean the guy looks like he stepped right out of GQ."

"Maybe so, but no need to stereotype, right? I mean, straight guys are capable of choosing their own clothes. Well, not Pete, but other guys. Guys who work in offices."

"Well, if that's not it, what could it be?"

"Maybe he's married," she said. "But that doesn't really make sense. That's not something people hide either."

"There's something, for sure. He keeps everyone at work at arm's length." I was really getting gossipy now. "Check this out. Normally, on the first of each month we get a cake at coffee time for all the birthday babies of that month."

"Seriously?"

"Yeah, yeah, I know… Office culture is weird. Anyway, so there's this enforced cake ritual and get this. He's been there for over a year now and not once has it been his birthday."

"Maybe he just doesn't want to participate in the enforced cake ritual. Do you guys have to sing Happy Birthday?"

"Sometimes."

"That's super weird."

"Focus, Claudia. Why wouldn't he want people to know?"

"Jehovah's Witness?" she offered.

"Nah," I said. "I've seen him drinking at office functions and he wished people Happy Hanukkah and Christmas last December."

"Maybe he's just private."

"Yeah, but why?" I was desperate. There had to be some reason.

"Some people are."

"I'm going to figure it out, mark my words."

"You do that, Super Sleuth. I have to get going. I have to read a whole other boring academic article tonight just so I can understand a footnote from the one I just finished. This PhD is going to kill me, I swear."

"You have to come out one of these weekends and blow off some steam. You must be going crazy."

"I am, but I don't have time."

"You and me both. I really ought to be focused on my career right now instead of dreaming about shagging my boss. I can't help myself."

\* \* \* \*

Later that night, I even went to our work website just to look at his face. His bio impressed me so much, I couldn't help but read it every time I clicked on his profile. He'd started a small business in his early twenties, got an impressive scholarship, graduated from Stanford business school, and entered the corporate world. Sitting in bed with my crush's face on my iPad, I realized just how pathetic my obsession had become.

The TV was on and there was an infomercial for a seminar on visualization. I got sucked in. Everyone in the audience wanted all kinds of ridiculous stuff—big cars, fancy houses, great vacations. Sure, all that stuff would be great, but the only thing I really wanted—the only thing that mattered—was true love. Great friends, too. I already had those. Claudia and Kristen were like sisters to me. And our other girlfriends were cool, too. I'd already achieved the big goal of my twenties—a beautiful home that I owned. I didn't need a car because I was right on the subway line and so was work. Besides, I didn't want anything I had to take care of. I had got a plant. That was good enough for me. Clothes—check. Awesome lifestyle—check. The only thing missing was Jerome.

The host of the show was talking about the law of attraction and how you needed to see something in your mind's eye before it could come true in reality. I propped the iPad up on the pillow next to mine and lay down beside it. Jerome's face was locked on a professional smile at me as I gazed into his eyes. I felt like a stalker. This wasn't working at all. What a scam.

# Chapter Two

I'd convinced Claudia to come with me to a company function I had been looking forward to. Claudia and I were dressed to the nines. We looked like two hot ladies ready for a night on the town. We were definitely fabulous. And I had wanted to get her perspective on Jerome for some time. But it was sort of a crazy night and I'd barely even seen her after we'd arrived at the event. It was packed with clients and colleagues, our board of directors and everyone's spouses. It was cool to work for a company that had such opulent celebrations, but the only real reason I was excited was that I wanted to see if Jerome had brought anyone and I wanted him to notice me.

I spotted him across the room, so I hurried toward him, leaving Claudia to talk with some of my co-workers. The queen I served — my nether queen, 'MiniMo' — was on a mission. From between my legs, she guided me to find him across the room.

I beelined for him, but just as I made eye contact, I noticed that there was a really pretty woman approaching from a different angle. She handed him a drink and he smiled when he took it. They seemed from afar to say 'Cheers' and took sips together and chatted and carried on. I figured she was the girlfriend. She had to be.

So I did what any petty, crushed-out nutcase would do. I stalked them. I casually inched closer and closer, weaving through the crowd like a cat, until I could hear their conversation. When I was within earshot, I heard the woman.

"My shoes are killing me. I have to go to the washroom to adjust my insoles. Let's hope I have some plaster for my blisters. I think I do."

The conversation was so intimate — and gross — that they had to be in a relationship. There was no way they didn't know each other really well.

I had this one in the bag. I waited until the woman had excused herself then I followed her into the washroom. I went through my purse, took out every bit of makeup I had with me and proceeded to reapply everything so that I'd be casually busy while she washed her hands. When she was drying her hands on paper towel, I said, "Great party, isn't it?"

"Yeah, not bad at all."

"Are you here with anyone?" I inquired.

"My husband. He works for the company," she said. My stomach threatened to flip over. I had expected her to say boyfriend, not husband. *Ouch.*

"That's nice," I said, trying my best to sound like someone who was just making conversation and not someone whose life suddenly felt like it had come to a crashing halt.

"How about you? Are you married to one of the suits out there?" Her smile was warm and genuine. Brutal. It'd be one thing if Jerome was married to some awful woman who was fun to hate, but a sweetheart? Worst case scenario.

"No, I work here," I told her.

"Oh, I'm so jealous," she said.

I was taken aback. She pulled out her lipstick and I noticed that it was Shiseido.

"I gave up my career to stay home. I sometimes wonder if that was a mistake."

I really hadn't seen that coming. Jerome had a trophy wife? That amazed me on many levels. "Well, whatever is the best for you, right?" I was trying to be vague but I think it came out wrong.

"Nice to meet you. Have fun tonight." She tossed her big blonde hair over her shoulder on her way out, like she was in a hair commercial.

How strange to think that Jerome had a woman like that at home. He didn't seem the type. My heart sank. I wanted to text Claudia to ask her to come to my rescue, but I figured I had to face the music. It'd look too weird if anyone noticed that we left after just fifteen minutes. I had to make it through at least an hour or two.

I gave myself a quick pep talk and pulled it together. When I emerged from the washroom, I saw the blonde again and this time she was on the arm of one of the guys who worked upstairs. Could it be that *he* was her husband? I thought that was the case indeed. She looped her arm in his. *Yes!*

Never in my life had I been so happy, so relieved.

*Back in action,* I thought to myself, looking around for Jerome.

I got myself a glass of pinot grigio at the bar. It would be easier with a prop in my hand. I was slowly circulating the room, nodding my hellos to the people I knew, greeting the faces that smiled at me. I walked around for what seemed like ages, performing all sorts of social niceties, complimenting people, trying to dazzle the higher-ups.

"Monique."

I turned, saw that it was Jerome, and with a strange loss of motor skills, I forgot to swallow the sip that was in my mouth. Instead I spoke, so wine dribbled out of my mouth and some of it went up my nose. The next thing I knew, I was coughing, trying to catch my breath. Jerome took my drink from me as I went into full-on panic mode. A woman in our near vicinity asked Jerome if I was okay or if she should call an ambulance.

"I think she'll be fine," he said and looked to me for guidance.

I nodded and continued to cough.

Jerome put his hand on my back and tried to soothe me. Embarrassing did not even begin to cover it. I wanted to slink out unseen, go to a hypnotist and have the last few minutes erased from my memory. How could I ever face him again?

Yet, there he was, right in front of me, wanting to make sure I was better. I finally stopped coughing long enough to convince him. "Pardon me," I said. That part came out right. But then I added, "I don't know what came—" And I meant to say 'over me', but I didn't get that far. I coughed again. My cocktail napkin was soaked. I had wiped my chin with it, blown my nose with it and held it up to my coughing mouth. I was a spectacle.

"Just focus on breathing," Jerome said. "In and out. In and out."

He was very reassuring, which was nice to know in case we ever ended up in a real medical emergency.

However, this catastrophe didn't qualify as a medical emergency.

"Let's go take a seat for a minute," he said. He took me by the arm and ushered me over to the seating at the sides of the room.

Some people who had been lingering there must have seen my debacle, because they got up so we could sit down. I began to breathe normally. "That was dramatic," I said, when I was able to speak.

Jerome put his arm around me and caressed my back. He looked right in my eyes and said, "I don't mean to sound unprofessional, but you look beautiful tonight."

What a lie! I looked like a fool. I looked like a drowned sewer rat with a red face from my own ridiculous episode. I could feel the tears that were streaming down my face. Awful, just awful.

"Thanks." I rolled my eyes when I said it, but I wasn't going to argue over the point. That'd just make it worse. "I should go."

"So soon?"

"Not soon enough." I got up.

"Don't go." He held onto my hand, keeping me in his reach. Perhaps he sensed how badly I wanted to bolt.

"Sorry you had to see that. And thanks for getting me through it."

"I'm sorry you're leaving early," he said. "Can't I persuade you to stay? These parties can be so dull."

If I hadn't already proven that the night was more than I could handle, I might have stayed. But no. It was time to go home. I had to find Claudia and get her. I prayed that Jerome wouldn't remember he'd seen me like that. I never had found out whether he was there with someone. It didn't matter. I felt like too

much of a dweeb to do anything even remotely sexy.
What a waste of a gorgeous dress. I shook my head as
I went to find Claudia.

"Let's get out of here," I said, but it was more of an
order than a suggestion.

Like a good friend, she performed the niceties
required of the situation—thanked my co-workers for
a lovely evening and grabbed my arm as I pulled her
out of there.

"Are you okay?" she asked out in the lobby.

"I'm a fool," I said.

"What happened?"

"Long story."

I filled her in once we were safely in a taxi headed
far away from there. What an awful night. Why was it
that the one guy I didn't want to look like an idiot in
front of was the only guy in the whole world who was
able to bring out my inner moron? It was a paradox
that I really detested.

"I think he really wanted you to stay," Claudia said.

"He was just being nice, trying to smooth things
over so I wouldn't feel like a dweeb."

"He meant it."

Why was Claudia taking his side? Couldn't she see
that he was doing the socially appropriate thing given
the situation? That was the kind of guy Jerome was.
He'd say the right thing no matter what. It could have
been Marjorie choking on her wine. He'd have been
sweet to her too. It didn't mean I was special in his
eyes.

# Chapter Three

On Monday, Jerome called a meeting in the boardroom to discuss the Murdoch file. There were six people, including me, on the file. I came last and the only seat left was the one right next to his. I hurried in, brushing gently against his arm as I passed him. It was like walking past a sweet shop with a beautiful display. I was tempted to take a detour, in this case to his lips. They beckoned me like chocolate éclairs. I couldn't help but smile. I was so scared that others would notice. He closed the door behind me and told me to have a seat. I hadn't seen him since *The Incident*, but if he remembered, he certainly didn't acknowledge it. I slunk in and took my seat.

"Let me start by saying good work to everyone. They like what we've done so far, but let's not forget — it's not enough to have them like us. This contract could shift the way our company docs business, so we all have a stake in this."

He'd looked right at me when he'd said the last part, as though he didn't think I took my job seriously enough, or something. I looked down and took notes.

Just then I noticed that the top button of my blouse was undone. How had that happened? If I did it up right then and there, everyone would notice. I waited until he excused us all then I bolted to the ladies' room. In the mirror I noticed that I was flushed. It was horrible to see myself this way at work. At home was one thing. I really didn't need any of the office snoops to catch on, especially Marjorie. She was such a Machiavellian.

\* \* \* \*

In the afternoon, Jerome made the rounds in our section and looked over everyone's work. I heard him tell Phillip, over in the next cubicle, that he'd done a great job of laying out the presentation. Marjorie was complimented for her extensive research. He called her resourceful. When it finally came to be my turn to have my work reviewed, he came around behind my swivel chair and looked at my screen while standing so close I could feel the heat from his body. I could have melted right into the chair. How was I supposed to listen to a word he was saying? Plus, he had just a slight trace of scent on him. It was nearly impossible to place but I had talent for this sort of thing. The cosmetics counter was my second home. It was something peppery and musky. My guess was Jo Malone. All I could think about was his bathroom at home. What did it look like? How did he look in the mornings when he shaved? How I longed to be there next to him, watching him from bed. I imagined he had an en suite, naturally. And maybe he kept his bottle of Jo Malone on his dresser along with his cufflinks, neatly arranged on a silver tray. He went the extra mile—that much was obvious. I mean, in this day and age, who even wore cufflinks anymore? This guy did.

"So, Monique. I'd like to see some adjustments."

Ouch. That was not what I was expecting. "What?"

"Well, you and I both know you can do better. This chart here, for example—" He reached over my shoulder and pointed at the screen.

I had barely an idea of what he was talking about since I was imagining the way his arm looked without a shirt on. I glanced to my right to check out the girth of it. It looked like he lifted weights. He was definitely built.

"So I'd like an updated version on my desk by Friday," he said.

I realized that he'd been talking the whole time and I had no clue what he had said or what he wanted from me.

"Okay," I said. "No problem."

With that, he tapped the back of my chair just slightly as though he wanted to pat me on the back but didn't. It was awkward and I had no idea how to interpret the gesture.

I looked up from my desk and caught Marjorie's menacing stare. She'd been eavesdropping this whole time. I was livid, until I realized that it was a blessing. At least someone had been listening. Now all I had to do was figure out a way to get Marjorie to tell me what Jerome had said. Who was Machiavellian now?

\* \* \* \*

I was down in the mall after work, getting my nails done, when I saw Jerome. I was waiting for the LED light to dry my shellac polish but I wanted, more than anything, to run out after him so I could follow him unnoticed. I really was turning into a Super Sleuth, as Claudia had put it, minus the *super* part. I resisted the urge to investigate. Besides, I wasn't about to get a criminal record for it. Better to stay until I had paid for my manicure. I watched him through the crowd. He went into a bookstore across the way. What could it mean? I wouldn't know unless I knew what book he was buying, but how could I find out? Was I really so crazy that I would stalk my boss in a shopping mall? It seemed a new low, even for me. I tried to concentrate on my nails. They looked great. There is nothing like new polish to make a girl feel bold. I paid the esthetician and tipped her well.

Just as I was leaving the manicurist's, I saw Jerome emerge from the bookshop with a bag. He turned right and, like a horse wearing blinders, he made his way out of the mall, not stopping to look at anything else. I couldn't help myself. I followed close behind.

Every time he turned, I was convinced that he'd see me. I had none of Nancy Drew's talents. I was a terrible stalker. But I had managed not to get caught so far, so that was something. When we had walked ten blocks together, I realized that Jerome wasn't going home. That's when it hit me that I wasn't sure I was ready to find out where he was going. How would I feel if we were headed toward a girlfriend's house? Then I'd be the pathetic loser I felt like, for sure. There'd be no denying it. And if there was one thing I still had going for me, it was denial.

Only Claudia knew about the crush. To anyone else, I could forever cover up the truth, even to Jerome himself, if he did turn out to be married.

I turned on my heels into the subway station and went home. *Forget it,* I told myself.

While I was on the platform waiting for the subway, I noticed a guy staring at me over his newspaper. He was trying to act casual, but I knew he was looking. I purposely looked the other way. Once we were on the subway, it was standing room only and I grasped onto a pole in the center. He jostled his way closer and closer until he was holding onto the same pole. Still I refused to look at the guy. I had a feeling about what was coming and I wasn't in the mood for it.

"Hi there," he said. "I don't normally do this sort of thing but I noticed you from afar and I know I'll regret it for the rest of my life if I don't tell you that you're stunning. I mean absolutely stunning."

"Thanks," I said, somewhat stiff-lipped. I just wanted him to go away.

"You must get that all the time."

I shrugged. "Not *all* the time."

"Well, you are very beautiful."

"Thanks," I said again. I had to admit that his compliment did soften the blow of the horrid experience I'd had chasing my holy grail. I smiled to show him a little appreciation. Big mistake. It is so easy for guys to misunderstand smiles.

"Like I said, I don't normally do this sort of thing, but would you like to have coffee?"

"Um," I said. "My aunt's in town."

He looked confused.

I added, "I mean, I'm menstruating."

"Oh," he said. "That's okay. It's just coffee."

"It really isn't." I had to keep the lie up now that I'd started it. "I have terrible cramps and I just want to go home."

"Some other time then?"

"Yeah... No," I said, shaking my head. He was sweet and all but I was not about to go for coffee with some dude who didn't know me at all and who had just stalked me from across a crowded platform.

Hmmm, I thought. Now there was a familiar scenario. It gave me pause. What had I been doing following Jerome? There is nothing hot about being followed. It is creepy and weird. And even though I hadn't been able to help myself these past few times, I had to take a vow with myself to stop it. Or else I'd be like this guy in front of me right now, the guy I'd turned down. I did not want to be this guy. My conscience wouldn't let me be rude to him.

"Listen," I said. "You seem really nice and it's nothing personal. I'm just... Well, I'm not looking for anyone right now. I'm sorry."

"Okay, well, like I said, I just knew I'd regret it if I didn't tell you that you're beautiful. Anyway, here's my stop."

He jumped out as soon as the doors opened. I wondered if it actually was his stop or if I had cruelly broken his heart and left him with a feeling of abject hopelessness. That was how I felt. Hopeless.

* * * *

I tried to distract myself. I really did. I worked out at the gym every day before work, trying to give myself some other form of outlet. I even said yes when this guy Jack called and asked if he could take me out for dinner. He reminded me that I'd given him my number at the pub the other night. Dinner's pretty high-level commitment in my books, and normally I'd put a guy like Jack in the coffee category... Maybe. But I was desperate. MiniMo was on my mind all the time and I knew that while Jack and I really had nothing in common, he was the kind of guy who'd put out and not make a big fuss about it. I needed a good old-fashioned hook-up. If I wasn't going to have Jerome's heart, I could at the very least have Jack's attention.

So after work, I went home to change and redo my makeup, going for the sultry look, specifically the 'I'll take you home and have my way with you' look. I wanted my eyeliner and smoky eye shadow to beckon to him, without looking like I was interested in getting involved emotionally. Just to really drive the point home, I wore my dark purple mini dress with the low-cut front and my black boots. My mother would have killed me if she knew I was going out with a guy I barely knew dressed like that. Heck, she'd have killed me for wearing that outfit at all, even inside my own four walls. But sometimes a girl's gotta do what a girl's gotta do. Jack picked me up at seven as he had promised.

When I opened the door, his jaw dropped. Literally. I was pretty pleased with myself for eliciting this reaction. And in the light of the autumn evening, he was a lot cuter than I remembered. *Maybe I wasn't that drunk when I gave him my number.*

"You look gorgeous," he said. "I mean absolutely incredible."

*Not a bad start.* "Thanks."

"Shall we?" He gestured for me to take his arm.

Suddenly, I had a different inclination. "We could go out," I said. Then, lowering my voice, I added, "Or we could stay in." I raised an eyebrow to seal the tone — just in case he didn't catch my drift. MiniMo was in charge. There was no denying it.

"I'm game," he said. He must have caught that he sounded like a frat boy, because he added, "Anything you like."

"Come in." I opened the door. "We can order something."

"I'm not really that hungry."

"Cool. Me neither," I said, tossing my jacket over the edge of my couch. I wouldn't be needing it any time soon. "We could always go out or order in after… I mean…later."

I was out of my mind, clearly. I was used to thinking things like that but not saying them out loud. This guy was caught in MiniMo's web and he was about to experience a different kind of date. It had been a while since I'd done this—taken a guy to use as my very own personal sex toy—but he seemed a good match for a few hours of fun.

"You have a great pad," he said. Again, he sounded like a frat boy.

"Thanks. Can I get you a drink?"

"That's okay. Maybe just some water."

"All right," I said, heading to the kitchen. One way or another, I was going to have some wine.

"Here you are." I handed him a glass of water upon my return.

He had taken the liberty of turning on some music, meaning that he had scrolled through my music files, which wasn't exactly a turn-on. Generally, I think of gadgets as private space, so a guy going through my music is like a guy going through my purse—a huge no-no. But again, I wasn't reading the situation from the brain. MiniMo was in charge.

He had taken a seat on the couch and his jacket was on top of mine, draped over the edge. I sat down next to him and took a sip of chardonnay. He'd clearly figured out exactly why I'd asked him in because he put his hand on my knee. I touched his hand.

"You're really hot."

"Thanks."

Then he leaned back, unzipped his jeans and unbuttoned the top of them. Slowly he pulled out his dick. It was already pretty hard.

*Um, seriously? No kissing? No chit-chat?* This was getting to be too porn-like, even for me.

He started to stroke himself while looking at me, as though he was silently asking me whether I could really resist.

For some reason — maybe I was horny to the point of sexual frustration, maybe I was simply being a good hostess — I went for it. In hindsight, that probably sent the wrong message, but at the time, I guess it was just awkward having this big, hard dick right in front of me. Talk about the big white elephant in the room.

So I slid down on my knees in front of him. He leaned forward and grabbed onto my breasts through my dress and bra. I was glad I hadn't taken anything off because he actually grabbed me kind of hard, but I let it slide. He reached for his iPhone, and I thought maybe he was sending a text message or receiving one. Either way, I'd never experienced anything quite so rude before, so I stopped and sat up.

"What are you doing?"

"Can I take some photos? Or, like, video footage?"

"What?" I was totally taken aback. "No!" I yelled. I was incredulous. "If I hadn't stopped, were you seriously just going to turn on your camera and film this?"

"You looked so hot. I thought you'd want to see."

"Oh my God." *What a pig!*

"I'd have let you keep the footage. It's not like I was going to put it on my porn blog or anything."

"You have a porn blog?"

"A Tumblr account."

"Oh my God. I can't believe it. You asshole."

"Whoa. Whoa. I'm not an asshole."

"You're the very definition of asshole, buddy," I admonished him. "Listen. I'm going to set you straight on a few things. When a girl invites you in, she's interested. That much is true. But, dude, life is not like porn. Real girls want a little more foreplay. Conversation. Kissing."

"I told you you were hot."

"That doesn't count."

"I'd have kissed you. I just figured you should make the first move."

"Well, I was thrown off by your dick out in the open like that. In the future, that's where you let the girl make the first move. You motion to kiss. The girl motions for your penis when she's ready. *If* she's ready. And you never, never pull out a camera on her." I shook my head. For some reason I felt more like my mother than I ever had before. I remembered the kinds of dressing downs she used to give when I was little and got into trouble. I sounded exactly like her. "And another thing. Who the hell taught you that it's okay to grab a woman's breasts like that? They're not clown noses. Come to think of it, I doubt clowns appreciate it when people go for their noses."

"I thought you wanted me to pay attention to them."

"Attention, yes. Be treated like some kind of carnival sideshow? No."

"I'm sorry." Finally! Those words. That, at least, was progress. Maybe he wasn't a total savage.

I shook my head again and motioned for him to put his flaccid penis back into his pants. "This should have been so easy. I was seriously ready to fuck you if you were even remotely fuckworthy. That's how easy this could have been for you."

"Can't we start over again?"

"Seriously?"

"Can I make it up to you with dinner?"

"I've lost my appetite."

He got up to go, took his jacket over his arm then slowly walked to my door like he was Eeyore and I'd just given him the worst night of his life. I really didn't appreciate his moping away like all of this was my fault, like I was somehow too choosy. I was not choosy. I hadn't lied. I would have fucked pretty much anyone yet he'd managed to turn me off. It was a wonder.

"Hold on," I said. "Let me ask you something."

"What?"

"Do you watch a lot of porn? Is that where you got these ideas about women from?"

"Yeah, but mostly homemade stuff."

"Show me that Tumblr account of yours."

"What?"

"I'm serious. I'm about to do you a huge favor. And I'm not just doing this for you. I'm doing this for every girl you go out with from this moment on."

"What are you going to do?"

"I'm going to put you through Monique's Sex Academy. Crash course. Starting now." I'm not sure what came over me, but since he'd managed to kill my mood, I felt like it was my duty to deal with this properly.

"I…uh… I don't know."

"Let me ask you this. How many girls have you been successful with?"

He looked down at his feet. "How did you know?"

"Dude…" I said. "Let me get changed. We'll order in. I'm about to change your life."

"Are you going to have sex with me?"

"No." I started out of the living room. "I'm going to do something even better for you. Sit back down."

"Okay."

\* \* \* \*

An hour later, we were eating Chinese delivery and going through all of the footage he'd found on the Internet and had collected on his Tumblr account. I had changed into my track pants and a T-shirt.

"Okay, let me ask you this. What percentage of real women shave or wax their pubic hair?"

"Um…all?"

"Erngh," I made a sound like a game show buzzer. "Wrong! Actually only about twenty percent and they usually don't keep it that way all the time. It's a special occasion thing."

"Really?"

I nodded. This was fun. "When did you start watching porn?"

"I don't know. I guess I was about thirteen."

"And how many women have you actually slept with?"

"A few."

"Long-term relationships?"

"Only one, when I was in high school, and we didn't have sex."

"So those few women… They were casual hook-ups?"

He nodded. "Well, I wanted them to be more, but…"

"But you busted out similar moves to what you did here a little earlier."

"I guess."

"Well, tip number one. Real girls do not appreciate being treated like porn stars. Real girls want to feel respected. Real girls want to take it slow, even if they mean to put out in a no-strings-attached sort of way."

"I do respect girls. Seriously. I have a lot of respect for women."

"Well, pulling your penis out—or your camera—doesn't show respect."

"I guess not."

"Put it this way... Would you like me to take non-consensual photos of you going down on me? And would you want me to have them in my phone where I can do whatever I want with them, like put them online or show them off to my friends?"

"No."

"So don't do that."

"I get it. It was an asshole thing to do."

"Ah. We're making progress. Have some more chow mein. Next question. How long does it take a real girl to come?"

"I don't know. Maybe a few minutes."

"Erngh! Wrong again. Most girls take at least twenty minutes or more and most girls need a lot of good clitoral stimulation—like her own hand or her vibrator. Reverse cowgirl isn't a good position for most girls to get off in. That's a big porn myth, too. There's no clitoral stimulation going on. And when you see men groping women's clits in these videos, they're doing it too hard."

"How do I know how hard?"

"You ask."

"That easy?"

"That easy. Girls want to tell you. They want you to know. So don't go in thinking you have all these moves—that you've learned from porn—just ask her what she likes and what she wants."

"So these scenes are pretty much all fake?"

"Yeah. Chances are you haven't seen a real orgasm. Sorry, dude."

"I feel like my world has fallen apart."

"Good. That means you can start over again in the real world. You'll probably do way better."

He looked into my eyes, so sweetly. "Thank you for this. It has been painful, but you really did me a favor."

"Like I said, I did it for the women in your future."

He leaned in like he wanted to kiss me. He even closed his eyes.

"Uh... Nope." I leaned back. "Sorry. You blew it with me, but you'll do better with other girls, I'm sure."

He shook his head like he was in utter disbelief. "So you really would have had sex with me earlier?"

"I was totally ready to."

"Man, I have to work on this. Two of the girls I slept with I really liked. I wanted to date both of them, but after our one time together, neither one of them ever called."

"You need to watch some *Sex and the City* and read some books by women on pleasing women. You're not a bad guy. You've just been corrupted by porn."

"I can't believe it's all fake."

"Not all of it. Go find some of the stuff that's made by women for women. You'll see. It's different. All right, time for this real woman to call it a night."

As I walked him to the door, he once again tried to convince me that I should kiss him, but I couldn't. MiniMo was desperate, but there was just no way to stoop that low, to be the first girl this guy was going to treat like a real woman. I cursed porn as I waved him goodbye. What a tragedy. He was cute and I was so ready.

Oh well. I would chalk up the night to doing a good deed. I had done a good turn for my sisters, so maybe I could expect a karmic reward in the form of a man who knew what he was doing some time down the line. I went back to my chardonnay, curled up on the couch. Maybe it was time to bust out a little of that feminist porn I'd extolled the virtues of. I had a couple of Candida Royalle videos in my collection. MiniMo craved some attention.

Out came the vibrator and I gave myself the attention I had wanted for so long. It's silly that the truth about women's orgasms is so foreign to a lot of guys, at least guys like Jack. As I vibrated myself to my happy place, I had an out-of-body experience. It was as though I hovered above myself and enjoyed the vision of this self-servicing woman who needed neither penis nor emotional connection in order to get herself to bliss. This was the very image of the modern woman — entirely independent. All I required were electricity and a handy gadget. I wondered if guys like Jack had any idea what they were up against.

# Chapter Four

When I woke up the next morning, I realized that I was glad nothing had happened. I'd been ready to hop into bed with any guy just to feel a man's body again. But if that had happened last night with Jack, I'd have regretted it. First of all, it clearly wouldn't have been very good. But more importantly, he wasn't Jerome. It was that simple. I knew as I got ready for the day—torturous work—that no man would compare. I could keep going out to the bars and trying for a cheap roll in the hay, but I'd never be satisfied. And that only led me to a more depressing thought— how long could I pine after Jerome?

I finally saw what my girlfriends had told me my entire adult life. I was a privileged and lucky girl. This whole time I'd had every guy I'd wanted. I'd never even had to try for it. A simple batting of eyelashes had usually done the trick. A nod or a smile in a certain direction. An offered phone number. A dropped hint that I wasn't dating anyone. It had all been so easy.

And it hadn't been until Jerome had entered my life that I'd seen what a curse ease could be. I'd only ever thought of it as my girlfriends did—a blessing. But really what I didn't have was the skill set to get my man. I knew nothing about working for it. I was hopeless. I was totally clueless.

I checked my mail on my way out of the door. I'd neglected it the night before and this must have come then. In my mailbox was a small envelope from Kristen, one of my dearest friends since high school. She'd since gotten married, moved out of town, bought a house with her husband and now there was this envelope. I hadn't even had my morning latte yet, so I didn't want to know the contents, though I had a pretty good idea of what came next after husband and house.

I went to Starbucks, picked up an extra-large skimmed milk latte then headed for the subway. It was packed and I managed to spill on myself as I tried to balance the latte in my cradled arm that also held my briefcase while I fumbled with the envelope. I was invited to a baby shower. Of course I was.

I thought about how Kristen had always been the lively one in our little group and how, after she'd effectively left us for her domestic life, I had sort of taken over her role of always instigating the girls' nights and having our gang of friends over. Had I secretly behaved like Kristen in an unconscious effort to get what she had? They haunted me, these morning thoughts. I was looking forward to the distraction of a day of work.

I never wanted a baby. The idea of popping one out of my vagina scared the hell out of me and I had no idea how women did it. Now Kristen was about to. She was the first friend I knew to make this announcement. Other people had had kids, of course, but I didn't know them very well, so I'd never had strong feelings about it. Kristen's invitation gave me pause. It made me feel like my life wasn't on track. Not exactly.

There I'd been the very night before giving a blow job to a guy who was so beneath me it hurt. I was glad I had been the Good Samaritan who had set him straight about how to treat women, but sheesh. Was this really my life?

I thought back to our high-school gang and what my goals had been then. Twenty-seven had seemed so far away—ages away. I'd figured I'd be married, have a meaningful career, be happy and successful. And I guess I was happy and successful, but there was no marriage in sight and my career was only so-so. I'd wanted Jerome's job. I still wanted Jerome's job, if I was honest. I needed a promotion. I needed to prove my worth as an analyst. Filling in spreadsheets was one thing. I had a lot more to offer. I hadn't graduated top of my class in business for nothing. Yet here I was, three years after getting hired, still working as an assistant.

To make matters worse, the guy I was assisting couldn't give me any guidance without my panties getting wet. I could barely understand him. Whenever Jerome spoke to me at work, I got tongue-tied and I couldn't concentrate. This was a tragic scenario and I finally saw it as such. It was awful.

And now, to top it off, I'd have to go put on a brave face and celebrate Kristen's awesome life. It's not that I wasn't happy for her. I was. I had been one of her bridesmaids—now that had been a wedding!—but it was becoming clearer and clearer that I was nowhere near what I wanted in my own life.

* * * *

I stepped off the elevator and the first thing I saw was Marjorie's scowl.

"You're late," she said.

I looked at the clock. "Three minutes."

*Who does she think she is?*

"I need your password to the spreadsheets for the Murdoch file. Jerome's taking you off the project and giving it to me."

"What?"

"Yeah. Come on." She walked me to her desk. It was as though she'd been waiting by the elevator just so she could do this. What a horror of a human being. "You can log me in on my computer."

"Um, maybe I'd better talk to Jerome about this first."

"Go ahead. He's just going to tell you what I'm telling you."

I went to my desk and put my coat over the back of my chair. I set down the remainder of my latte and considered popping a mint before talking to Jerome, but I wasn't even finished yet. Why did this morning of all mornings have to be so hideous?

Jerome's glass door was closed, but he saw me approach so he got up from his desk and opened it for me.

"Come in," he said. "I take it Marjorie talked to you?"

I nodded. "She can't be serious."

"Have a seat."

*Damn. This is not good.*

"Listen," Jerome began. "This is the least pleasant part of my job so I'm just going to come right out and say something I probably should have said months ago."

My own soundtrack ran something like— '*You're in love with me?' 'I know! Me too! We don't have to hide it anymore!*'

But that was not what he said.

What he said was, "You're exceedingly bright, Monique, so don't take this the wrong way, but I've come to the conclusion that it'd be better if you were not on the Murdoch file."

"Are you serious?" I asked. A million defenses were ready to come out. I wanted to tell him why he was making a huge mistake.

"Wait," Jerome said. "There's more."

"Okay," I said hesitantly.

"I think your skills will be more useful in another department."

"What?" I cried out, perhaps a little too loudly. "Where?"

"It's a good switch. It's not a demotion or anything. Think of it as a promotion. I've discussed you with Stuart upstairs and he is confident he can use your skills and creativity."

"Creativity?"

"You are better suited for a more thinking role than an administrative one, wouldn't you agree?"

"Well, yeah. But..." *I don't want to transfer out of this department. I don't want to be on a different floor from you. Don't send me away!*

"So it's all settled. They have a desk set up for you upstairs and you're even getting a new computer. I think this will be a great step forward for you."

"So, that's it?"

"What do you mean?" He looked surprised, as though he had expected me to humbly capitulate.

"I've been terminated by you."

"Not exactly."

"Why are you getting rid of me?"

"Monique, I think we both know that you'd be better off elsewhere."

*What the hell is that supposed to mean?* I wondered, but I didn't dare ask. I was feeling naked enough as it was. Did he know I was in love with him? It sure felt like it, like he could see right into my innermost core. It drove me crazy, and in that moment, it made me sadder than I'd been in a long time.

"So I guess we won't see much of each other anymore," I said. "Well, uh, good luck with everything." I got up, turned on my heels and lurched for the door.

"Monique…"

"Bye."

I didn't want him to catch on that I was on the verge of tears. I didn't want anyone to see, but of course there was an entire open-plan office floor of faces looking in my direction, as tended to happen any time someone was asked to sit down behind that glass door.

I approached my desk and did my best to think about puppies and unicorns and anything that'd make me not cry.

"Monique," Marjorie said. "Can I…?"

"Don't talk to me," I cut her off. Immature, yes, but it couldn't be helped.

I took out a pen from my top drawer and scribbled the password on a Post-it note. *Screw her. Screw this entire department. Screw Jerome. Just screw it all.*

I left my things in the drawers. I could come back at a less humiliating time to empty my desk. They had to allow me at least that dignity. And I was nowhere near ready to face Stuart and a whole new job description. I put on my coat, picked up the remainder of my latte then went to the elevator. Instead of pushing the button to go up, I pushed the one that would take me down into the mall.

Sometimes, the only way to deal with life is to get a pedicure. So there I was at nine fifteen in the morning at Serenity Spa checking out the colors. I selected a bright coral color, something cheerful. Anything to make me feel better. Then the esthetician led me to one of the chairs specifically designed for pedicures with the built-in sink attached. She poured in some crystals that turned the water blue and I immersed my feet in the warmth. I did feel a modicum of improvement for a minute, but then the unthinkable happened.

There was Jerome, standing in the middle of the nail spa. He must have followed me. He looked totally out of place and out of breath.

"What are you doing here?"

"When I saw you didn't go up to the seventh floor" — he panted — "I took the stairs down. I didn't like the way our meeting ended. I wanted to make sure you're okay."

"Well, I'm not."

"I was afraid of that."

As though there was nothing peculiar about this interaction in the slightest, the esthetician sat down on a stool beside the basin and took my left foot into the towel she had placed on her lap. She soaked a cotton ball in solvent and proceeded to take off my old polish.

"I just need to take a moment to adjust to the news," I said. "I didn't realize I was so expendable."

"You're not."

"Clearly I am."

"It's nothing personal, Monique. Believe me. If I could keep you on, I would. I just can't afford the risk right now."

"Am I really such a terrible employee? I'll have you know before you came, I was at the top—I got better results than all of them. Better than Marjorie." I said her name with a sneer. It was awful. Totally unprofessional of me.

"Well, listen, it's not you. It's me. I think it'd be better if you worked upstairs."

The esthetician submerged my left foot in the water again then took out my right foot. The polish remover felt cold on my toes.

"What? Why?"

"I can't get into it."

"Okay-ay," I said slowly. "So what you're saying is you don't want to work with me anymore."

"That's not it. I don't want you to leave with that feeling."

"Well, that seems to be precisely what you're saying."

"Then I'm failing miserably."

I'd never seen him look so vulnerable before. Suddenly, right before my eyes—and my esthetician's—he went from being the ambitious corporate hard-ass to being a puppy dog, and I couldn't take it. No matter what his reasons, I had to let him off the hook.

"I'll get used to the new job," I said. "I've just never been fired before."

"I didn't fire you. I had you transferred."

"Fine. Transferred. I've never been ousted from a job before in my life. My career is the main focus of my life, you know? And I pride myself on taking my work seriously."

"You're good. No argument from me there. I think you'll be happier in Stuart's department, actually. He told me about the work he needs you to do and it sounds like there's some serious room for advancement. And by the way, your new job does come with a salary increase."

"It does?"

He nodded.

"So I was actually promoted?"

"Yes."

"Why did it feel so awful then?"

"I'm not sure, but that's why I ran after you. I didn't want this to be hard on you. It wasn't meant to be. It was meant to improve your career, not hinder it."

"Okay," I said feeling shy and embarrassed. "Then thank you for my promotion."

"You're welcome. Congratulations."

"So I guess I'm getting this pedicure to celebrate and not to cheer myself up."

"It's a lovely color. Your feet will look great, I'm sure."

I blushed. "Uh, thanks." This was suddenly unbelievably awkward. Like terribly awkward.

Jerome kept standing there, like we were frozen in time. I no longer knew what to say and, clearly, neither did he.

"Well, don't stay down here too long. I know they're anxious to get you started," he finally said. "As for me, I'd better get back." He motioned to leave.

"Jerome?"

He lunged back like he'd been attached to elastic that had snapped abruptly. "Yes?"

"Thanks. For coming after me and making sure I was okay."

"No problem. It was my fault you were upset. It was the least I could do."

"It was kind."

He smiled. "Well, you're kind."

I smiled at the compliment, and with that he turned. Over his shoulder as he left he said, "I'll see you up there."

"Sure."

*What the hell just happened?*

When my toes were done, I went upstairs, shook Stuart's hand and was greeted by my new department. It was a promotion—Jerome was right. I was on the seventh floor instead of the sixth, and I had a better desk. It was bigger and it faced the window instead of the corridor view that I'd had downstairs. My computer screen was bigger and brand new. And there was a better coffee system up here—an espresso machine with little pods that could generate instant lattes and cappuccinos. Not bad at all.

And without Jerome around, I might actually be able to get some work done, I figured. So it wasn't entirely awful. But it was. I went on the company network and stared at Jerome's little green icon that signaled he was available for a chat. It would be entirely inappropriate to instigate a chat with him since we had nothing work-related to discuss.

Or did we? I dug deep. Surely there had to be something. Anything. Anything at all.

That afternoon, I sent him a message.

*Just want to say thank you.*

To my utter surprise, he responded two seconds later.

*No problem. How is your new desk? Are you enjoying the big monitor?*

*I am. You knew? Are you behind this too?*

He sent a very unprofessional emoticon—a winky face.

*;-) Enjoy your promotion, Monique.*

I could barely breathe. I had to actually fan myself with a paper file folder. It was too much. I pictured him winking at me and wondered how that would feel. MiniMo had a reaction, too. I could feel my panties get instantly wet, which was so wrong and so unprofessional. It was torture of the worst kind. Not only did I not get to see Jerome anymore, but I had these strange messages to decode. What did it mean to receive a winky face from him? I'd never seen that kind of thing in his correspondence before. Never in his emails. Never anywhere. Would he have sent a winky face on a message to Marjorie? Or was I justified in interpreting this message as something special?

Oh, the torture.

# Chapter Five

The green light next to his work avatar haunted me. It meant he was available. If only it were true. I thought back to the first time I'd seen Jerome. I'd been prepared to dislike him before I'd even met him, since I'd been mad at him for taking what I had already decided was *my* job. I had applied for it, interviewed for it, almost gotten it then Sinclair had taken me out for the world's most awkward lunch. He'd started out by saying it was supposed to have been my celebratory lunch, but that at the last minute a different, more qualified, person had swooped in and impressed the higher-ups. Who was this guy? Someone middle-aged, I'd presumed. I'd been wrong. He was none other than fresh from Stanford, the ambitious young entrepreneur-turned-corporate executive Jerome Fontaine. He'd been written up in Metro Business Monthly for his humble beginnings as a sandwich maker and how he'd taken the Stanford business experts by surprise. I'd been convinced that I was going to hate him.

Then, on the morning he'd started, he'd showed up with a cooler full of sandwiches for everybody. It was his way of introducing himself. He'd explained how his grandfather had had a hot dog stand and he'd grown up helping out. How his dad had gotten to go to college because of the hot dogs and how he, too, had gotten to go to an Ivy League school all because his grandfather had been willing to get up each day and feed people their lunch.

It was a pretty moving speech he made. I'll never forget it. He stood up in the middle of the office and told us that he'd had an identity crisis halfway through college because he wasn't sure he wanted to be in big business, so he had gone to see his grandfather, who told him to get his hands dirty. He launched a sandwich delivery business in the summer and paid for the remainder of his college education that way. Then he said he knew he could do small business and suddenly big business was appealing, which led to his applying for the scholarship. Then he said something that I still find perplexing. He said, "Always do what you love and if you don't love what you do, then do it for the people you love."

I never forgot it because I wondered then—and still do now—what he meant by it. He was clearly pretty passionate about the sandwich business—and he made excellent sandwiches—so who was he working for? Why had he dropped the small business to take a corporate gig?

I'd been immediately smitten with him, the way he'd entered the office like he owned it, the way he'd had this down-to-earth story to tell everyone, the warmth of his descriptions of helping his grandfather when he was little. The caramelized onion and brie sandwich hadn't exactly hurt, either. All of it had seemed so genuine, but then as the days and weeks had passed, I noticed that he'd zipped up about his background. That was all we got, just that first introduction.

Then there had been that strange incident around Thanksgiving last year when Paul from my old department had talked about volunteering at the soup kitchen downtown and Marjorie had mentioned that her husband's family was flying in to spend the holidays with them and everyone had started talking about their plans. Jerome had asked me if I had anyone special to spend the holidays with, and I'd said that I was going to spend it with my mom. He'd smiled and told me he thought that was nice, then had asked me to describe my favorite dish. I'd told him about my mom's tarragon turkey, how she grew the herb in her backyard and every year she'd hang up a bunch and dry it out, then at Thanksgiving she'd use it on the turkey. It was so special knowing she grew it herself and put so much care into it. The whole house smelled divine because of it. Jerome's eyes had lit up when I'd told him. It was like he understood exactly what I meant, like maybe his family had similar traditions. I'd asked him what he was up to that year, hoping he'd divulge a little, but he'd said he was going to spend it with family. I'd wanted to ask what he meant by that. Family is such a vague word. Anyone from siblings to parents, spouses or second cousins qualifies. So what had he meant? The more I thought about it, the more I recognized that he had been cagey from the first moment I'd met him. Yet, somehow, he'd always seemed to manage to get me to talk. I told him everything.

The really odd part—frustrating because of just how sweet it was—was that a couple of weeks later, he'd showed up at work with a big grin and had called me into his office.

"Got something for you," he'd said. He'd tossed me a Ziplock bag of dried tarragon and told me it was from the community garden where he volunteered sometimes.

I had wanted desperately to hear more about his volunteer work—was he some sort of spare-time farmer?—but his phone had rung and he'd made it clear that our conversation was over.

It was incredible just how distracting that little green light of his could be. I had to get work done.

Stuart and my new colleagues upstairs had made me feel welcome and they even took me out for a welcome lunch. We went to a cute new bistro called Le Cochon. The guy I'd be working closely with, Stephen, said he'd thoroughly enjoyed my presentation in our interdepartmental meeting a few months ago.

I pushed him for more details, wondering if he could shed light on precisely how I could contribute my skills up here, since I still wasn't entirely clear on the matter.

"You were captivating," he said.

"But what…exactly?" I needed more.

"You have a really engaging presence. I could listen to you for hours."

"So… Public speaking?" I clarified.

He nodded. "Stuart should really get you to give presentations to clients. We'd probably do much better."

"You don't think it's best if the head of the department does them?" I mean, that was sort of the golden rule around here. Let she or he with the most authority speak directly to clients. Jerome always handled clients personally.

Another guy, Todd, backed him up. "You do have good stage presence," he said.

It was then that I noticed that my new department was made up of men exclusively. And they were all paying attention to me, watching me and smiling. It was dizzying. A younger me would have found it intoxicating and exciting, but in a way, it just felt like a relief. None of them threw me off my game. None of them were elements of distraction. In fact, it was great when Stephen brought up my public speaking skills in front of Stuart—who, it was true, wasn't the world's most dynamic presenter—because he nodded his approval.

"To an excellent addition to our team," Stuart toasted with his Coke.

We all clinked glasses. An auspicious beginning.

"Thanks," I said, making sure to make eye contact with all five of them.

Stuart added, jokingly, "We're all looking to you to get us our Christmas bonuses."

*What?* I smiled. "Bonuses?"

"Sure," Stephen said. "Every year, if we increase productivity by some specific numbers, we get an additional percentage each." He took a sip. "I can show you the pie charts when we get back to the office."

"Done and done," I said. Nothing pleased me like the word bonus. It gave me something to focus on.

It was silly, really—my obsession with money. I already made, at the age of twenty-seven, more than my parents had made from both of their jobs while I'd been growing up. I suppose that's where the incentive came from. I didn't want to replicate the lifestyle I was used to back then. I didn't want to stretch between bills or worry about the future. Besides, it felt great to be in a place where I could treat my mom to luxuries she was not accustomed to. If only Dad were still here. I'd have loved to have sent them on vacations. As it was, Mom and I had managed to get down to a sunny resort each winter for the past few years. That meant a lot.

When we were back in the office, I started crunching numbers. Could I take this group to the next level? I believed I could.

\* \* \* \*

The weeks passed smoothly. I threw myself into work and tried not to think about the heart-throb who worked on the floor beneath me and who stealthily made his way through my department like a wolf, once in a while. Sightings managed to give me flushes and, since I was driven to turn my new department into the highest yielding one Porter & Sons had ever seen, I felt grateful that I didn't see much of him.

But MiniMo was capable of no such feeling. It was late. Most of the office building was dark. Only we workaholics were left. I had been singular in my focus for at least two months at that point, living and breathing a huge file, which, if we landed it, would secure not only bonuses, but would also likely pave the way to another promotion for me. It was ambitious. It was huge. It was scary and I had become a ball of tension ever since I'd decided to pursue it.

When the elevator stopped on the sixth floor, the doors opened to reveal Jerome. My heart pounded. Immediately, I bathed my teeth with my tongue, and fixed my hair. Why hadn't I bothered to look in a mirror?

He stepped into the elevator with me and pushed the button for the parking garage. Then he looked at me and smiled.

"Monique Mackenzie. Wow."

I couldn't help but smile. What did he mean by that?

"How are things, Jerome?"

"Downstairs? Good." He shrugged as though to suggest there was nothing new or exciting going on. "Not as exciting as what's going on in your department."

"What do you mean?"

He nodded just once in a secretive manner. "Oh yeah, that's right. The person who is the talk of the town rarely knows."

"What?" I had no idea what he meant.

"You. You're all anyone talks about. I might actually be given a bonus for promoting you. You're on fire."

"You...heard?"

"Oh yes. I had a feeling that moving you would be the best thing I ever did."

*That's it. It's now or never. You only live once, right?* So I said it. "You don't miss me?"

He looked sheepish, which was an unfamiliar look for him. "I didn't say that."

Our eyes locked. I wanted the elevator ride to last longer. Why couldn't we work in a taller building? Instead, the doors opened on the ground floor to reveal the mall that connected our building to the subway station. This was my stop. I started to go.

"Well, have a good evening," I said.

A woman with a paper shopping bag got onto the elevator. We passed each other.

"Wait."

"Yes?" The elevator dinged. The doors started to close, but Jerome pushed the button that caused them to stay open. The woman looked at him.

"Would you like a ride home?"

"I don't live in your direction," I blurted. *Oh my God, I sound like a stalker.*

"That's fine. I'm heading south," he said.

"Sure." I stepped back into the elevator.

We stood, the three of us, in silence for the final descent. How did he know what direction I lived in? I was sure I'd never mentioned it. How on earth did he know?

The elevator doors slid apart. The woman went her way. Jerome motioned for me to go first.

"I don't know what kind of car you drive," I said. "You'd better lead."

"Fair enough. Ladies first isn't always the most practical."

He walked beside me as we rounded the bend to where his dark blue Prius was parked. He clicked his keychain to unlock the car. He walked around to the passenger side and opened the door for me. I got in. He closed the door for me.

When he was in, I said, "Nice car. Hybrids are great."

He smiled. "I don't have anything to prove in terms of speed."

"That's awesome. I hate guys who drive fast."

"Here's a little secret about men. They usually do that because they're trying to impress a girl by scaring her just a little bit."

"Well, it doesn't work on me."

"I'll keep that in mind. Always obey speed limits when Monique Mackenzie is in the car."

It was intoxicating to hear him say my full name. That was twice in fifteen minutes and my ears were burning. MiniMo was excited beyond belief. It felt like the temperature inside the car was through the roof. I wanted to roll down the window but I didn't want to draw attention to the tiny beads of sweat that I could tell were forming along my brow.

The car had that nice new car scent and one quick glance revealed that Jerome kept it very clean.

He turned the key and the radio came on, only it was a CD and it was the last thing I'd expected. It sounded like some kind of kids' music. He switched it off immediately.

"What was that?" I asked.

"Nothing. Nothing."

"No, really. What was it? It sounded like *Sesame Street*. Big Bird, to be specific."

"Um…" His lips tensed. He put his right hand up to his brow as though he was trying to come up with some sort of rational explanation.

I ejected the CD from the CD player. It was, indeed, *Sesame Street. Elmo and Friends Sing-a-long*.

"What's this?" I laughed. "Jerome Fontaine, is this how you motivate yourself for corporate presentations?"

"Something like that," he said. Chuckling, he took the disc from me and put it in the compartment beside him on the driver's side door.

What a strange turn of events. I really didn't know what to think.

He changed the topic abruptly, "So, what's the best way to your place?"

"Truth be told, I never drive in this city. I'm not sure."

He turned on his GPS system. "What's your address?"

I told him and he punched it into the car. "That's so close to where I'm going," he said.

"Oh?" *Where are you going, you mysterious man?*

"Mm-hmm." He pulled out of the parking spot, and we circled, slowly, around to the parkade's exit.

I was nervous. Jittery. I had butterflies in my tummy. This was the last thing I'd expected, to spend time with him in the privacy of his car. I'd done such a good job of censoring myself around him at work that I couldn't quite believe we didn't have to be careful not to be overheard by the likes of Marjorie and Paul or other snoopy co-workers. I had no idea how to start conversation with Jerome. It was such a strange feeling. No man had ever brought this side out in me. I was tongue-tied. So I said nothing and neither did he. We drove in silence for several minutes.

"Do you mind if we make a quick stop up ahead?" Jerome asked.

"Of course not," I said.

He pulled over, put the car in park and told me to make myself comfortable. I wondered if that meant that it was okay to open his glove compartment. Rationally, I decided it wasn't an open invitation to spy on him, but I had never felt so tempted before. I looked around, and his car was the perfect representation of him. Everything was locked away in compartments. There was no mess, not so much as a fallen hair or anything to inspect. The car was just as mysterious as the man. How frustrating.

He returned carrying a white box with pink floral print and lettering on it. The top was clear cellophane. He opened my door and placed it on my lap.

"Would you mind holding onto this?" he asked.

"No problem," I said. Finally. Something to see.

Beneath the cellophane was a blue and green birthday cake with dinosaurs on it. It read, '*Happy Birthday, Aidan*'.

Jerome sat down beside me. I said, "Awww. What a cute cake." It was an invitation to tell me more, but Jerome offered nothing.

Instead, he said, "Yeah, they do a good job at Katrina's Bakery."

"I'll keep that in mind," I said.

He launched into an analysis of Katrina's business plan, how the bakery had originated as a neighborhood cake shop and how Katrina was amazing because she really fostered a connection with the community. For ten minutes he went on and on about the great outreach program she had, how she donated day old pastries and bread to various shelters. I almost got the sense that he was into this lady, but then he said it was extra impressive because she was a grandmother and her aging husband was in and out of chemotherapy. I wondered how he knew all that, and whether he was friends with the family. His eyes had that same look that they'd gotten when we had talked about Thanksgiving. Maybe he was just really into food.

Then it occurred to me that it could be a trick to deflect attention from this supremely odd situation we were in together—alone—in his car, *not* at work. It was incredible how stoic Jerome could be. Like, really amazing. I couldn't help but want to pry, but I knew better than to push him. I could tell from a mile away that he was not the sort of guy who liked to be pushed. And anyway, I was in this for the long haul. Better to exercise patience. So instead of asking whether Aidan was the real fan of Elmo and friends, I decided to take the conversation in a different direction.

"So, do you ever miss the sandwich business?"

"Oh, you remembered."

"Of course. It's not every day a new boss shows up in the corporate world and talks about catering."

"I wasn't your boss."

"Manager," I corrected. Why was he being such a stickler?

"To answer your question, yes. I miss it," he said. "But you can only shirk responsibilities for so long. I've got different priorities right now. This gig pays a lot more."

"So you're not doing what you love, but you're working for the people you love?"

"Do you have a photographic memory? Is that how you're able to advance so fast in the ranks?"

"Maybe I do," I kidded. *For what you tell me.*

"Well, you're doing something right. You've got yourself perfectly poised for a major advancement. You know that, right?"

I nodded. I did, in fact, know. It had only become clear in the past few weeks, but it was clear. "I'm doing my best."

"It's impressive."

"Thank you."

As we pulled onto my street, I realized that he had magically evaded answering my question about his work motivations. This guy was way too smart for his own good. I wondered if they'd taught him how to be elusive at Stanford or whether it came naturally.

"Here we are," he said, pulling over in front of the heritage building where I lived. "Nice place," he said.

"Thanks. I have the top floor."

"Nice. Balcony?"

"Yeah, in the back."

He shook his head. "They don't make houses like they used to. Looks like you've got a good set-up. Do you get garden access?"

"I can use the backyard if I want to, but I'm not a gardener."

"That's too bad," he said. I wondered what he meant by that. Why was it too bad?

"I like my balcony," I said.

"Do you have a barbeque up there?"

"As a matter of fact, I do."

"Nice."

"It is. I should have you over some time."

"I do love barbeques," he said. "Thanks for taking care of the cake."

"No problem. Will you be okay getting it to your destination?"

"I'm sure it'll be fine."

"Thanks for the ride," I said.

"Any time."

As I exited the car, I agonized over the abrupt end of our contact. How many weeks would pass before this would ever happen again? *If* it would ever happen again. I shook my head as I walked up to my door. He stayed in the car until I waved from inside that I was home safe. He waved back and drove off. I hoped he hadn't noticed the way I'd shaken my head.

\* \* \* \*

From the safety of my living room, I called Claudia and filled her in.

"He is beyond frustrating."

"You're in love."

"Is this what love is?" I asked. "It's messed up."

"Awww, Monique," she teased. "I've never heard you like this."

"I've never been like this."

I shook my head at myself. I had it bad. Even though it was a week night and I was alone, I broke my own rule and opened a bottle of merlot. Desperate times called for desperate measures.

"What is it about him?" I asked. "Am I so screwed up in the head that I have to fall for the most emotionally unavailable guy I know? Am I a masochist?"

I told her about the other guys I worked with, how I got the sense that the single guys in my department would go for me in a second if I wanted them—not to be arrogant. I caught myself telling the story and I sounded arrogant, even to myself. "But you have to understand," I said defensively, "I don't care about any of them. I only care about Jerome."

"Welcome to love, Monique. You've never felt like this before, have you?"

"Not even remotely."

Claudia laughed. I told her she had to come to my office function in a couple of weeks. She had to see this guy. I needed her to assess whether I was crazy or not.

* * * *

One Friday evening, I took the elevator down after work and Jerome got on. It was just the two of us.

"Exciting plans for the weekend?" I asked.

"Yeah, actually." He faced me. "We're holding a big fundraiser where I volunteer."

"Where's that?"

"At the Sinclair Park Community Garden," he said. "I'm head of their outreach program. So, hey, if you've got any old cooking utensils or pots or pans you no longer use, feel free to bring them by."

"When?"

"I'll be there all day tomorrow and half of Sunday, so any time."

"I have some plates and glasses I've been meaning to throw out."

"Don't throw them out. We can use them in our program."

"All right. I'll see if I can fit it in," I said. I didn't want to sound too eager.

"It'd be nice to see you," he said.

I blushed and looked down, not wanting to meet his gaze. He cleared his throat. The silence was excruciating, but I didn't want to tell him it'd be nice to see him too.

When the doors opened, I said, "Maybe I'll see you tomorrow."

"Good," he said.

* * * *

On Saturday afternoon, I took the subway to one of the inner city parks. Carrying a box of old kitchen supplies, I walked toward the community garden. There, in the blazing hot sun, with his shirt off, was Jerome. My, oh my, how sculpted he was. I knew he'd be built, but I didn't know just how built. His muscular arms did not look like those of an office worker's. For one thing, they were tanned.

"Monique!" he said when he saw me. He rested the spade he'd been holding against the fence.

"Hey," I said. "Where can I put this down?"

"I'll take it." He looked concerned as soon as the box was in his grip. "This is heavy. You should have called first. I could have carried it for you."

"It's fine."

"Well, let me show you around, so you know about how useful your old stuff will be for us. This here is the community garden, as you can see."

"Wow." It was huge.

"These are the potatoes, turnips and beets. Oh, and carrots. I grew all these myself."

I followed him as we walked. He pointed to the other side. "Over there, we've got the herb garden, tomatoes, peas and corn."

"Is this where the tarragon came from?"

"Yes. I grew it myself."

"You didn't tell me that when you gave it to me."

"Didn't I?"

"So you volunteer as a farmer on weekends?"

"Something like that. We're lobbying the municipality for more space. We're teaching kids from the inner city how to grow and cook their own food, so we need all the space we can get."

"Wow, Jerome. That's impressive. I had no idea you had this side to you."

He shrugged. "I don't like to talk about it too much at work. It scares the suits."

I was incredulous and didn't know what to say. One of the other volunteers, a teenage boy, came up to Jerome and asked about watering. Jerome's attention was immediately on him as he gave the kid instructions.

He turned his attention back to me. "There's nothing more important for young folks than to know their place in the ecosystem, to get their hands dirty and remember that they're part of something much larger.

It's so easy to feel cut off when you grow up in the city, buying produce imported from Mexico and whatnot. They come here, learn about growing vegetables and it gives them a whole new perspective. Come on—let me show you the kitchen."

"Impressive," I mustered. I followed, totally flabbergasted.

Inside, a girl in a bandana with two long braids hanging down each side of her face looked up and greeted us. "Hey, Jerome, I sorted the beans like you told me and then I moved on and did the peas."

She had piles of little kernels in front of her and a basket for the husks.

"Great work, Sasha," he said, putting the box of my old stuff down on the counter behind her. "This is Monique, my friend from work."

We waved at each other.

"Are you here to help cook for the fundraiser?" she asked.

"I don't even know about it," I admitted.

"We're hosting a community supper tonight. The mayor might come," Jerome said. "At the very least some of the parks board commissioners will be here and we need their support if we want to keep the after school programs running."

"I don't know what I'd do without this place," Sasha said. "Anyway, I gotta go compost this. Be right back." She took the basket with her.

"This is incredible."

"It's a start," Jerome said. "It's nowhere near where I'd like it to be, but Rome wasn't built in a day, either. Next step is city support. After that, investors."

"And then?" I was so curious about his plans.

"One step at a time," he said.

Even on the weekend, Jerome didn't divulge much.

"So, you coordinate?"

"I do everything. I give cooking lessons. Tonight we're making lentil soup, fresh herbed buns and a potato and chickpea curry."

"Wow," I said. "I gotta hand it to you—this is not what I thought you did on weekends."

"You won't let the cat out of the bag at work, will you?"

"Of course not," I said. "Your secret is safe with me. Though I don't understand why you keep it secret."

"I have my reasons," he said. "Well, I should probably round up the troops and get these guys started."

It was my cue to leave.

# Chapter Six

A couple of weeks later, on a Saturday afternoon, I got dressed in my best party outfit—a sweet green and blue dress I'd bought some time ago on a spree at the outlet mall. I'd been looking for an occasion to wear it and Kristen's baby shower was just the thing. I did my makeup and checked myself out. Sure, I didn't have everything I thought I'd have by now, but I was no pity case, either.

I grabbed a cab.

"Where to?" he asked.

"Babies 'R' Us on Broadway, please."

"All right."

We drove in silence, and I looked out at the city I'd known my entire adult life, a city I loved. I thought about all the possibilities that still existed for me. I felt entirely optimistic and I was happy for Kristen that she was living her dream. I was living mine in my own way. And maybe mine would never include a baby, and that was cool, too. My mom had long ago let me off the hook with that. She'd told me she didn't see me as the maternal type, which, at the time, I'd taken as an insult, but it wasn't. It was acceptance. I felt grateful for her.

The cab driver pulled over and I gave him a good tip. I was really in a great mood. I even popped into Starbucks and grabbed a Caramel Macchiato, a rare treat. Why not? This was a festive occasion.

Hot drink in hand, I sashayed through the aisles trying to figure out what Kristen would need. I didn't want to buy her diaper-related stuff or breast pumps. Nothing related to body functions was my motto. Maybe something in the bath department. That seemed like a good idea.

Somehow, because I wasn't really paying attention, I found myself in there. Out of the corner of my eye, I caught a slice of an image, barely enough to be totally sure, but it was unmistakable. Jerome. It had to be. I could recognize his gait anywhere. He had a very special way of walking. He carried himself with confidence.

Stealthily, I grabbed a disguise off the shelf. I huddled behind a giant stuffed koala bear as I took careful steps in the direction of my vision. It was like being in a cartoon with a lampshade on my head and it worked. Sure enough, it was Jerome. And he was not alone.

He was there with a woman. If she was a girlfriend, she was a surprising match. She had short-cropped hair and she was wearing overalls. She looked a little like Peter Pan, though slightly more feminine. Was it jealousy talking? I wasn't sure. My heart pounded. I didn't want to get caught spying. That would be a disaster, but I had to see what they were buying. I had to figure this out.

They strolled casually through the aisles laughing and joking around. They were close. That was for sure. But were they lovers? It was hard to decode. They really didn't seem suited to each other. But then, before I knew it, I had advanced with the koala as my front all the way to the sporting goods section where they stood debating about bikes.

Still with my Macchiato in hand and my purse over my shoulder, I crept toward them, ducking behind the aisle near them, hoping I'd be able to overhear.

"Need any help, ma'am?" a young girl wearing an oversized Babies 'R' Us T-shirt asked.

"Uh... No," I whispered. "Thanks."

"Okay," she said, somewhat sarcastically, like I was a crazy woman.

Well, I was creeping around, hiding behind a giant stuffed bear. I couldn't blame her for judging.

When I concentrated, I could make out the words.

"He'll love it," the woman said. "But it's too much, Jerome. Let's not spoil him."

"Come on. Just picture his face when he sees this in the driveway."

"He would be ecstatic."

"Let me buy it."

"I'm not going to tell you what to do."

"Good." He reached up to the top shelf and pulled down a small shiny blue bike. "We should get training wheels, too—and a helmet."

"You're a great dad," the woman said.

And that's when I couldn't help but take a step back and exclaim, "What?"

I backed into a display of boxed and stacked soccer balls. The soccer balls toppled a pile of hula hoops that went skidding across the laminate floor. Toddlers and children wept out of surprise and all eyes in the store turned to me. There was nowhere to duck, nowhere to hide, so I tried to run away, but I tripped over a neon pink hula hoop. Disaster. I'd been holding onto the koala but let it go as I crumbled to the ground. The bear went on to knock over an arrangement of boxed games.

As if that wasn't enough, I skidded and landed on my butt. My Caramel Macchiato went flying and spilled all over my dress and the floor. An announcement came over the loudspeaker almost immediately. "Clean-up in Sporting Goods."

"Monique?"

I didn't look up. If I didn't look at him, maybe he wouldn't see me. Maybe he'd think it was some other crazy lady.

"Is that you?" he asked.

"No," I said.

By then he had come over to me, and I saw his outstretched hand in front of me. Still sitting on the floor in a pool of lukewarm coffee, I turned and looked at him. I bit my lower lip and tried my best not to cry.

He laughed. "What are you doing here?"

I took his hand and stood up, instinctively trying to brush the coffee off my dress. It was hopeless. I was soaked.

"Uh… Shopping?"

"For soccer balls?"

"I'm quite sporty, I'll have you know."

He nodded. "I didn't know."

He saw right through me and laughed. Then I burst into laughter, too. I looked around at my surroundings. I had created a complete catastrophe. The poor young folks that worked here would have to spend hours wiping down the coffee-splattered toys. Yikes. This was worse than the time in Grade Eight when I'd dropped my tray full of macaroni in the high-school cafeteria. Way worse.

The woman he'd been bike shopping with came over.

Sweetly she asked, "Are you okay?"

"Yeah," I squeaked. *No, no I'm not.*

"I'm Bev." She offered me a handshake, like this was a most natural way to meet.

"Bev, this is Monique," Jerome said.

"Ah." She nodded. "Monique from the office."

I nodded. "That's me."

She knew about me?

"I've heard so much about you," she said, as though to answer my question.

Jerome shot her a look like she'd spoken out of turn.

"I mean, not *that* much," she corrected.

Jerome shook his head, glowering at her. It was a relief not to be the only person who was embarrassed.

Like he could always be counted on to do, Jerome changed the subject, "Did you hurt yourself when you fell?"

"I'm okay," I lied. It felt like my entire backside was bruised.

"So were you really buying a soccer ball?"

"No, I'm going to a baby shower. Just picking up a gift," I said. "But I guess I'll be going home to change."

The manager of the store came over to see if I had hurt myself. He seemed relieved when I said I was fine. It was as though his face expressed the joy of no impending lawsuit. But he raised a different issue. "We can't sell that koala bear anymore. It's soaked with coffee."

"Fine, fine," I said. "I'll charge it. And a gift basket with baby products."

"Okay," he said. "What would you like in the gift basket?"

"I don't care," I said. "Anything."

"Price range?"

"I don't know." I felt suddenly overwhelmed with Jerome and his Baby Mama and/or wife or girlfriend standing there watching. I saw the birthday cake in my mind's eye. Their happy lives flashed before me. "Whatever. A hundred bucks?"

"Sure thing." He turned to go. "Is it for a boy or girl?"

"I have no idea," I said. *Why so many questions?* I was a pathetic mess of a crazy lady who was in love with a family man. How could I be expected to know the gender of the recipient of the basket? Besides, Kristen hadn't specified. "Just some bath towels and bath wash and stuff like that. That'd be just fine. Anything you come up with will be fine."

*Just go away.* I was projecting. I wanted nothing more than to go away. Disappear. Undo the last five minutes of my life. *Breathe, Monique, breathe.*

"Can we give you a lift home?" Bev asked, looking me up and down.

"No, that's okay," I said. There was no way I was going to be able to hold back the tears for long. Jerome was raising a family with this woman. Nothing could be more painful than this.

I realized I'd be lucky if I could excuse myself without bursting into tears, so I hurried up. "I...uh... I really have to go. It was nice to see you, Jerome. Nice to meet you, Bev."

I picked up the huge koala bear and held it around its neck. As I turned to go, I felt like I was a toddler myself. I buried my face in the bear and cried as I dashed away. This, by a landslide, was the low point of my life. If I looked at my life's trajectory, this was rock bottom. Nothing worse. Nothing.

When I was out of their line of vision, I wiped my tears with my sleeve. Everywhere I looked, shoppers stared at me. There was nowhere to hide in my wet dress with this giant stuffed animal. I'd had nightmares that were kinder than this.

When I approached the counter, the clerk was just wrapping ribbon around an oversized basket of baby paraphernalia. "Would you like a card?"

*So many questions.*

"Sure. Whatever."

*Just get me out of here!*

I swiped my credit card and left. Out on the street, it felt impossible to get a cab. Several went by me without stopping. This was what it boiled down to. The big difference between the crazies and the rest of the population, and I now knew how I was perceived. Then I saw that the koala had black marks on its face. I fumbled through my purse, pulled out my compact mirror and saw, to my horror, that, yes, in fact, I did have black mascara stains running down both cheeks. Pathetic.

Just then, I felt a hand on my shoulder. Jerome was behind me.

"Are you sure we can't give you a ride?"

"Go away," I said.

"Monique, come on," he insisted in a calm voice. "You can see the humor in this, can't you? I mean, I know your dress is probably ruined but…"

"Dress?" I snapped. I turned around. "You think I'm upset about my dress?"

"I…uh… I…" He backed off and put his hands up like I was about to make an arrest.

"I don't give a shit about my dress, I'll have you know."

"Okay, okay," he said, maintaining a really even, calm tone.

"You broke my heart, okay? You happy now? You wanna know why I'm upset? I'm upset because I just finally came to the very clear conclusion that I've been living in some kind of messed up fantasy bubble of my own creation."

I was just getting started. I could feel the emotion in me boiling over and there was nothing I could do to stop this outburst. So I continued, "I'm so stupid. Here I thought you had a cute little nephew or something, but no. You have a family."

I advanced toward him, owning the crazy lady construct, accepting it. This was the real me now. Let it shine. There was nothing left to lose now that every smidgen of pride was gone.

"And another thing... What kind of manipulative mind-fucker puts emoticons in professional emails? This is not entirely my fault, you know. You led me on."

The koala came at him and I used its right arm to do the pointing for me.

"You know what, Jerome? I see through you. I know exactly what you were up to at the office party now. I'm on to you. And if you think I would ever have an affair, you're way crazier than I look."

"Whoa, whoa. Monique, calm down. You've got this wrong." He shook his head at me.

"Oh, so I suppose I just made up that you were flirting with me?"

He took the condemning koala from me and set it down on the sidewalk. "Monique, Monique," he pleaded in his steady, calm voice. "You're not wrong about that. But you are wrong. Let me explain. Hear me out. Please."

"Don't you have to be somewhere…with your wife?" I spat the words at him. Take that.

"Bev is not my wife," he said. "And, no, she took off already. I'll catch up with her later. Can I take you home so you can change? Maybe we can talk there?"

I capitulated. His soothing tone did a number on me. Besides, I was tired of yelling. I only have a few minutes at most of yelling capacity and I've only ever had a few such outbursts in my life. I'm not a very good fighter normally. I guess it just all got to be too much and I snapped.

"Sure, take me home."

"Do you want to keep this guy?" He lifted the koala bear up from where it had been seated on the ground.

I shook my head. "I don't know what to do with it," I said.

"Let's take him with us," he suggested. "For now."

I nodded. We walked to the parking lot beside the store. Jerome opened the passenger door to let me in and put the koala in the back seat. He strapped a seatbelt around it. It almost made me laugh that he would do that. Maybe I had blown things out of proportion a little, but I was very confused.

"You're not turning on the GPS?" I asked.

"I remember how to get to your place," he said. "It's really close to here."

It was mere minutes, and Jerome knew a shortcut.

We left the koala in the car and he carried the gift basket upstairs behind me. I opened the door. "Come on in."

He looked around and bent down to take his shoes off. "Nice place."

"Thanks," I said, kicking off my heels. "I can hear you from the bedroom if you sit on the couch and project your voice. Start talking." I walked down the hall and into my room.

I was aware of the anger in my voice. I had to let him know that I had not exactly forgiven him yet. There was a good deal of explaining to do.

"All right," he said, taking a seat on the sofa. I took my dress off as soon as I was safely out of sight. I was feeling cold from the wet coffee and it was a relief to be out of the dress.

He started, "So, I have a son. His name is Aidan. He's six."

"I got that part. Why aren't you with the mother?"

"Bev? Bev is like my sister. She was my high-school sweetheart but that was a long time ago."

"Sounds incestuous."

"I'm not finished. We went to Prom together, and I lived with her in San Fran while I went to Stanford. We shared an apartment."

"So far not sounding overly 'brother-sister' if you ask me."

"I'm trying to tell you we go way back. Just let me finish. So anyway, in the first year, she realized she was gay and we broke up. But we kept living together because, well, San Francisco is expensive and we still loved each other, just not like that. Then she met Cole and they've been together ever since, even after I moved back here, and when they wanted to start their family, they came to me."

"Seriously? Was there a threesome or something?"

"Are you kidding? Hell no. All they wanted was the sperm. In a cup, I might add." He stopped and, like the Jerome I'd come to know, tried to change the subject. "Did you know that buying sperm can cost a couple over ten grand? It's a serious hindrance for lesbians who want to start a family."

"Back to you, Jerome."

"Okay. So anyway, the deal was that they would raise the kid and I'd get to see him or her when we all got together, but they'd be the parents and the kid would never know that I was the dad. I was twenty-three at the time and didn't think much of it. Just jerked into a cup like I said I would and handed it over. They had their happy love nest in San Francisco. I flew out when Aidan was born and again a couple of years later. They decided to move home before he started school and when he got to kindergarten and all the other kids were talking about Mommy and Daddy, he had a lot of questions. So it was then—last year—that we all sat down and decided it was best to tell him straight up."

"Really?" I had put on a stretchy cotton dress and came out to watch him tell me the rest. He was sitting crouched over, like it was painful for him to finally tell me the whole truth.

"Yeah. And when we told him, his face lit up and you know what he said?"

"What?"

"He said, 'I always knew you were my daddy'." Jerome got tears in his eyes when he told me this, and I couldn't help but put my hand on his arm. I sat down beside him. I was getting misty too. "Well, ever since then, I knew I had to step up and be a daddy."

"Is that why you took the job at Porter & Sons?"

He nodded. "If I took a good corporate job, he'd have benefits and tuition later."

"What about Bev and Cole?"

"They're good providers, don't get me wrong. I mean, they give him the most caring home a kid could want. But Bev teaches yoga part-time and Cole delivers the mail, which used to be a good union job but the government is practically laying off posties these days."

"So you stepped up. And sacrificed your dreams."

"I don't think of it as a sacrifice. I think of it as taking care of my family, doing something I'll be proud of when I look back at my life. I'll get back to the sandwiches. Believe me. Actually, with the salary I'm making now, I've got my eye on investing in a food cart when the time comes. Like my granddad had, but different. You can get them with heat and everything nowadays."

"But I still don't understand why you're so cagey about it at work."

"I'm private, Monique. I always have been. You know the way Marjorie and Paul and those guys get all involved in everybody's private affairs—gossiping and whatnot. That's not for me. It never has been. Besides, I made myself available for potential transfers and promotions. If they knew I had a kid, they might not give me the high-paying contracts. And the truth is, I can only handle a few years of working in the corporate world. It's not really my thing. So the way I see it, they can send me to the moon if they're willing to pay me top salary. I only want to give them a few years of my life. Then, once I've made enough to set up Aidan and myself, I'll throw in the towel and do what I love. So, yeah, that's my game plan."

"That actually makes sense." I'd found myself nodding along in agreement the whole time he'd been talking.

"Life has a funny way of working out. I mean, I never expected to be Aidan's dad. None of us expected it. But now I wouldn't have it any other way and neither would Bev or Cole."

"That's really sweet." I meant it. I was shaking my head in disbelief at all the conclusions I'd jumped to. Jerome was mysterious, but he was no liar.

"Yeah, we're a real modern family."

"As long as it works and Aidan's happy. That's really all that matters."

"Aidan is amazing. Do you want to see him?"

"Yes!" I said. "Of course. I've been wanting to see him ever since I saw the cake."

"He really liked that cake. Here. I've got a good one of him blowing out the candles."

He scrolled through his phone and found the photo. Aidan's cheeks were filled with air and his eyes beamed with joy.

"He's so cute!"

Jerome nodded. "He's incredible. Really. I'd like you to meet him."

"You would?"

He nodded. "Listen, there's still more I haven't told you and I've felt bad about it, but in my books, it's been family first, you know?"

"Yeah," I said. "I get that." I was scrolling through the photo album on his phone, looking at all the precious moments between Jerome and his son.

"Before I took that job, I had a stern talk with myself. I said, 'Jerome, no drama, no office politics, no nothing. Get your paycheck and get out'. And then I showed up on my first day of work and there was this goddess there. And I couldn't stop thinking about her. I'd wake up in the middle of the night after dreaming about her and it was torture, but I couldn't say anything or do anything because, well, you know the rules. Nothing creates drama and gossip like office romance. So I told myself to just cool it. Ignore it. Take cold showers. Anything."

My heart felt like it was going to explode. "So I wasn't crazy? You were flirting with me?"

"I couldn't help myself. I tried so hard not to."

I wanted to tell him it was mutual but I was having so much fun listening to this. So I just nodded and encouraged him to keep going.

"There's still more I need to tell you and I hope you won't be mad."

"Okay…"

"I had to transfer you. I couldn't be around you all day, every day. I couldn't even do my job. I could barely concentrate when you looked at me or when I walked by your desk or… Do you remember that time I had to show you something on your computer?"

"Yeah," I said. "And you leaned over my shoulder. I remember clearly."

"I can't remember a single damn thing I said. I could barely talk."

"Well, you did better than I did. I didn't hear a word you said. I was so distracted by having your arm so close to my ear and feeling the heat of your body behind me."

"So I wasn't alone in feeling like we had a moment then?"

"Oh, we had a moment," I said emphatically.

"So here's the thing. I went home that night and I did some soul searching and I knew that I could not go on like that. And that's why I had you transferred."

"I see. So it had nothing to do with my work abilities?"

"Well, it did. In a sense. I mean, I could tell you were cruising by a little too easily at work. You needed a promotion. It was time. I was surprised your last manager didn't put you up for one."

"Tell me about it. But she didn't know what she was doing."

"Well, I sure did. Not only was I able to do my job but get this... The higher-ups even gave me a bonus for seeing your potential and moving you up."

"Well, in that case, dinner's on you."

"So you're not mad?"

"Jerome, I've never been happier in my life. Honestly, the last couple of months in the new position have been the best I've ever had in my entire career. I mean, I love the corporate world. I hear what you're saying about politics and gossip, but I thrive on stuff like that. I love games. Maybe that's why I was so intrigued by you."

"You were?"

"You couldn't tell?"

"I wasn't sure. I've never been too sure about things like that. I'm terrible at reading the signs."

"Well, let me just say that from the first moment you stepped into the office and gave that speech about your granddad and the hot dogs, I was smitten. It was bad. I had it bad. Ask my friend Claudia. Of course, me being the cool veneer type, I didn't want anyone to find out, least of all you. So I tried to distract myself. Cold showers, like you said."

"For real? That works for women, too?"

"Well, I wouldn't say it works," I laughed. "But I was desperate."

"Monique Mackenzie, I can't believe what I'm hearing." He paused. "So are you free for dinner?"

"I have waited a long time for you to ask me that," I said. "Yes. I'm free."

"How about tonight? Not as a date-date. I'll take you out with the bonus money later. But tonight I'm going over to see the family. Aidan's getting a bicycle for his perfect report card."

"Wow! Perfect report card?"

Jerome beamed proudly and nodded. "I'd love for you to meet everyone."

"I'd love to, but first I have to…" I looked at the time. "Shit. I'm late. I have to go to Kristen's baby shower."

"Let me drive you."

"It's kind of far."

"I don't care."

"You sure?"

"Monique, I have been wanting to spend time with you for over a year. Let me drive you."

"I'm going to need to hear that a few times before it sinks in."

"I'll tell you until you can't stand it anymore."

Jerome was so different from the closed off guy I knew him to be at work. It was night and day. Here, on my couch, he was open and relaxed. He wanted me to meet his family. I thought about the events of the past hour and a half. It was surreal.

"Let me just freshen up and we can get going."

"You look beautiful exactly as you are right now."

\* \* \* \*

It took over an hour to drive out to the suburb that Kristen and her husband call home. I couldn't exactly ask Jerome to turn around and drive back home. I could have taken the train, of course, but he'd insisted that he was fine to tag along.

"I've actually never been to a baby shower before."

"Even Aidan's?" I asked.

"I wasn't in San Fran anymore and besides, Bev and Cole aren't into those cheesy games and whatnot. No offense."

"Hey, none taken. You think I want to spend my Saturday afternoon folding napkins into diaper shapes?"

"Is that what's about to happen?"

"I can't say. I don't know. All I know is that Kristen really is into this sort of stuff. And she's one of my old friends from high school. We go way back. So I sort of have to get into it."

"Well, let's do this thing," he said as he put the car in park. "What's Kristen's husband's name?"

"Steven, but I…"

"What?"

"I don't think he'll be here."

"This is an all-girl party?" He put his head down and rested it in his palm. "Oh boy. What have I got myself into?"

"Um…"

He shook his head, but there was an air of playfulness about it.

"You can go. I'm fine getting home alone."

"No, no. I want to bring you to my family." He paused thoughtfully then said, "Ah. So let's make the best of this."

"You're a good man, Jerome Fontaine."

"You can tell me that later, after I pass the test."

"Test?"

"I know what women are like when they get together."

When Kristen opened the door, she was wearing a diaper on her head.

"Come in!" She kissed both of my cheeks and whispered in my ear, "Who's the hottie? Please tell me you brought a stripper."

"Kristen, this is Jerome."

"This is Jerome?" she asked. She turned so he couldn't see her and mouthed silently, "*The* Jerome?"

I nodded.

"Jerome!" she squealed. "Nice to finally meet you. Come on in."

I gave her arm an instructive squeeze. She didn't have to be *that* obvious.

"Thanks," Jerome said.

We were ushered into the living room where a congregation of women of all ages greeted us in unison. Jerome was the only guy.

"Hi," he said. "What game are we on?"

"Diaper crowns," Kristen's mother-in-law said. "Best one wins a prize. Here—" She passed him a white cloth diaper, which he took as though there was nothing awkward about it at all.

Kristen held me back a moment. "He's so cute," she said.

"We haven't even been on a date yet," I said.

"And he's here with you? He's a keeper."

I smiled. He'd passed the first impression test with flying colors. Before we went in, Kristen whispered, "I would kill for a gin martini right now. I can't wait to have this baby."

"You and me both," I said, then corrected, "I mean, the martini part."

"Come with me," she said and led me to the kitchen. She gave me a champagne glass and took a ladle full of prepared mimosa out of the punch bowl. "Let me top it off for you." She opened the fridge and poured more sparkling wine into the glass.

"Auntie Minnie makes the weakest drinks in the world," she added. "Should I make one for Jerome?"

"I'll check."

I went into the living room and he had all the older women in stitches. There was a whole crowd gathered around him as he put together his diaper crown using some kind of elaborate folding technique.

"Jerome? Would you like a drink?"

"Sure. Nothing with alcohol, though."

"All right."

I went back to the kitchen and told Kristen what I'd seen. "You've got to see this."

We re-entered the party, and Jerome placed the crown on his head. The women cheered and laughed and clapped their hands. It was, by a landslide, the most impressive one in the room.

"How on earth did you learn to do that?" I asked.

"Simple. Origami."

"You know how to fold origami?"

"I was a bit of an awkward kid, okay?" he said. "Anyway, it's paying off big time."

Kristen's mother-in-law pronounced him the undisputed winner of the diaper crown game and handed him a wrapped box. It was pink and had a big bow on it.

"Thanks," he said and took a spot on the sofa next to Auntie Minnie. He started to unwrap it very carefully not to tear the paper.

Auntie Minnie's patience was wearing thin and she scolded Jerome in her eighty-three-year-old shaky voice. "Oh for crying out loud. Just open it," she ordered. She took the box from him, tore the wrapping off then passed the gift back to Jerome.

Inside there was a gift certificate. He held it in his hands and looked on both sides as though there would be an explanation on the card itself.

"Oooh, fifty bucks at L'Atmosphere," he said, sounding like he was very impressed and pleased with the prize.

The room burst out laughing. Auntie Minnie and all the other elderly ladies laughed so hard that some of them struggled to catch their breath afterwards.

"What?" He was so helpless and innocent.

"It's a lingerie shop," I said.

"O-oh," he said, blushing. "Well, then I think I might be the luckiest man to ever attend a baby shower." He winked at me.

The ladies stared back and forth between us.

Then, Auntie Minnie started a chant, "Kiss, kiss, kiss!"

The women who weren't too busy laughing joined in the chant. I got up from where I was seated and slowly walked over to Jerome. He was looking right into my eyes and smiling his warmest smile.

I kissed his cheek.

Auntie Minnie seemed displeased. "If I wanted to see that, I'd have turned on late night cable. I was expecting a little more from you, Monique."

"We haven't even been on a proper date yet," I explained.

She stared blankly, like I'd cheated her.

"Sorry," I said. "I'm saving the first mouth-to-mouth kiss for when we're in private."

"All right, all right," she relented. Then, as though Jerome weren't sitting right next to her and able to hear everything, she said, "Don't wait too long. This one's the marrying kind."

"Auntie Minnie!"

"What?" She shrugged. "I'm old. I know things."

# Chapter Seven

By the time we left the baby shower, Jerome had a dedicated fan club, and I'd gotten a number of private words from the elderly set. It seemed that everyone thought he was The One. Even Kristen's own mother, who generally wasn't too vocal about these things, had told me she'd never seen me so happy before.

When we got out, the koala was still sitting on the back seat strapped in safely with a seatbelt. This time the sight of it made me keel over in laughter. It came from deep inside my belly.

After he'd opened my door and closed it behind me, he got in himself. Then Jerome smiled and said, "That was fun."

"You were a great sport."

"I enjoyed myself." He reached into his shirt pocket and pulled out the gift card. "And this is for you. Best prize I've ever won."

I smiled and took the card. "You just wait."

"Oh, I am patient." He winked. "By the way, thank you for not kissing me in front of everyone for our first kiss. I really am on the private side."

"I understand. Me too."

"Besides, I wanted our first kiss to be longer than a quick peck in front of Auntie Minnie."

"Mmm-hmm," I agreed.

"Something kind of like this." He came closer.

I closed my eyes. His lips met mine and I felt goosebumps all the way from my spine to the back of my neck. In my head, I heard Cher singing *It's In His Kiss* and I knew it was. I knew. The women at the party were right. All this time, all these little clues and signals between us had led up to this moment. It all culminated in this kiss. What a kiss it was. His lips were so soft and warm against mine. He reached around me and held me in his arms across the gear shift. Sparks flew. Fireworks went off. This was perfect.

Then I opened my eyes and saw the crowd of women that had gathered in the meantime. They cheered. Even Auntie Minnie had come out, holding onto her cane for support. She wasn't going to miss this.

We burst into laughter and waved, like we were a royal couple.

As we drove off, they all waved back.

"I like your friends," he said. "Those ladies have pizzazz."

"They sure do."

"Ready to meet Aidan?"

"I am."

He took my hand and drove with only one hand on the steering wheel. My hand felt so good in his. His hands were one of the first things I'd noticed about him, how large they were and how the shapes of his fingernails pleased me. They were perfect ovals and he kept them neat.

I was feeling ever so slightly tipsy from the spiked mimosa, which was probably partly why my tummy felt like it was doing back flips. I was also trying to digest the day's events. How strange it was to think of all the misunderstandings that had taken place between us over the past weeks and months.

"Jerome?"

"Yes."

"I really like you."

He squeezed my hand. "You have no idea how good it feels to hear you say that."

"You must have known," I said, thinking back to how gushy I felt every time I saw him.

"I figured you knew, too," he said.

"I didn't," I admitted.

He shook his head and laughed, "Me neither." Then, when we stopped at an intersection, he added, "I figured a girl like you had tons of men all pining for your attention."

I blushed. "Well, let's not exaggerate. Not tons."

"A lot."

"Some." I paused. "But the point is that none of them meant anything. All I could think about was you."

"But you were dating. Are you dating anyone now?"

"I did go out with guys, yes. But only because what was going on between us felt so impossible."

"Don't get me wrong, Monique. I'm not jealous. I'm not trying to act possessive, either. I mean, up until a couple of hours ago, you didn't even know how I felt. I just thought I should know in case you had some other guy or guys in the wings."

"I don't. Do you?"

"Guys? Nope," he laughed. "I don't go that way."

"Girls?"

"Nah. My last serious relationship ended around the time Aidan came into my life. Just afterward. She was okay with me donating sperm, but she couldn't handle that I wanted to spend so much time with him after he was born. I felt for her. I mean, I didn't know that Aidan would change me so much. It was true that all my weekends went to daddyhood and before, they used to go to doing the stuff she liked to do. But that's parenting. It's not exactly romantic."

"I see," I said, suddenly preparing for the worst. "How long had you two been together?"

"Oh, not too long. Just over a year at that point."

"Was it serious?"

He shrugged. "I guess not. I mean, to me, a relationship is all about helping each other grow. Change is inevitable, right? But then when something big happened in my life, she didn't really want to accept the change. Plus, she didn't like kids. So I guess that was the deal breaker."

"Oh, so you broke up with her?"

"I had to. I mean, she told me she didn't care much for Aidan. So, what sort of future could we possibly have together?"

I stared out of the window. Gulp. I sure hoped I liked the kid.

"I'm sorry," he said after a slightly awkward silence. "I didn't mean for this conversation to take this turn. We haven't even been out on a date yet and I already told you about my ex. No wonder Bev calls me an honorary lesbian."

"Oh yeah?"

"Yeah." He nodded. "Outside of what you see at the office, I actually really like talking about feelings. I don't understand why most guys don't. It's helpful."

"Oh my God. That might just be the sexiest thing any man has ever said."

"It's true. And there's nothing wrong with a good cry now and then, either." He paused. "In private, of course."

Had he fallen from the heavens? I thought back to that night I spent with Jack and the good deeds I'd been doing lately. Maybe this really was my karmic due.

Jerome pulled into the driveway of a large brick house with two front doors. It was typical of the neighborhood—a renovation to turn a hundred-year-old house into an affordable duplex. The garden was kept neat and tidy, and there were planters all the way up along the stairs. It was obvious that the people who lived here cared a lot about their home.

I was on a high from the day so far. Jerome opening up about his feelings for me had me walking on sunshine. The day's magic made it feel as though my heart was enveloped in a glowing orange light.

As soon as the car was in the driveway, a tiny face appeared in the living room window and an excited little arm waved in our direction. Then, before I had even had a chance to check my lipstick and hair—I wanted to make a good first impression—the front door was wide open and a little boy was running toward us.

Jerome leaped out of the car and bent down. The boy jumped into his arms and the two did a twirl-like dance move that involved a pirouette and a dip.

Still inside the car, I heard, "Daddy, Daddy! Who's that lady?"

I stepped out.

"Aidan, this is Monique."

I waved. "Hi, Aidan."

He turned back to his father as though he hadn't registered my presence at all.

"What do you say when someone says hi to you, Aidan?"

But he turned away from both of us and hid his face in Jerome's neck.

"It's okay," I said. "He's shy."

"I'm not shy!" he insisted.

"Okay," Jerome said. "Then politely say, *Hi, Monique.*"

"No!" he said very firmly.

"Aidan," Jerome said, this time very calmly. "Be nice."

But instead, he started to cry. Maybe he was overwhelmed. Maybe he thought I'd steal his daddy away. Who knew? All that was clear to me was that this was not going smoothly. I was off to a bad start with his family and after he'd done so well with my friends. I had to make this right.

Jerome looked at me sympathetically and shrugged. He nodded toward the front door and turned toward the house. "Let's go inside."

"What's that?" Aidan asked, pointing to the koala.

"It's a big koala bear that Monique brought for you, but if you're not going to be nice to her and say hi, then she can't give it to you, can she?"

He shook his head. It was cute to watch the tiny wheels spinning.

Quietly, he said, "Hi, Monique."

"Hi, Aidan," I said.

But to Jerome I said, very quietly, hoping Aidan wouldn't hear, "But it has coffee spilled on it. Is that okay?" I didn't even mention the mascara or remind him of the fact that it had been on the sidewalk for a while earlier that afternoon.

"It's fine," he reassured me. "Don't worry."

"All right." I opened the door to the back seat and took out the bear. It was as tall as Aidan. "Would you like this koala bear, Aidan?"

He squirmed in Jerome's arms to signal that he wanted down. Once on the ground, he ran over to it and threw his arms around it.

"We have a winner." Jerome smiled, his face warm. "Come on."

Aidan tried to carry the bear himself, but he couldn't. Jerome picked up the bear for the second time that day. He sure knew how to save the day.

By the time we got up to the front door, Bev and Cole must have heard the noise, because they came to greet us.

Bev took charge and said to Cole, "This is Monique, you know, *from the office*."

This time, I was flattered. I understood what I didn't understand before, that Jerome had talked about me, that I existed in their imaginations before they'd even got to meet me. It made me feel so special and it made me desperately want to impress them. Nothing felt more important than having them like me.

"Hi." I extended my hand to Cole first. "It's so nice to meet you."

"We're huggers," she said. "Come here."

She threw her arms around me and gave me a hug. Then she backed away a couple of steps. "Whoa, whoa," she said. She looked at me like I'd offended her. "This is a fragrance free home."

"Cole," Jerome pleaded. "She didn't know. We didn't know we were coming here. It's spur of the moment."

"It's mostly on my cardigan, I think," I said. "I can take it off."

"That'd be good," Bev said. "Sorry to be rude, but could you just leave it in the car? We're both sensitive to perfume. Cole especially."

"I'm sorry," I said. "I'll be right back."

Jerome passed me his keys and I went out like a guilty dog that had just been scolded. Bad first impression.

Then I tried to unlock the car door the old-fashioned way. It had been a long time since I'd owned a car and back then, I'd had a key to get in and out, not buttons. The alarm started blaring. The horn honked. The lights flashed. I wanted to die. I thought I would.

Jerome came running. He grabbed the clicker from me and pushed the right button. The whole mess was over. He opened the car door, and I tossed my cardigan onto the passenger seat.

"I'm so sorry," I said to Jerome. "I'm off to a terrible start."

"Don't worry," he said, taking my bare arms into his firm grip. The palms of his hands reassured me. He whispered, "I don't know why they insist on hugging when they're allergic to perfume. Makes no sense." He shrugged and added, "Family."

I took a deep breath, and we walked up the steps together. Inside, we took off our shoes. I was down to nylons and my sleeveless dress in terms of clothing and the sun had already set. It was starting to get cold. But this was Jerome's family, I reminded myself, and I'd waited so long to be here. A little chill meant nothing.

"Thanks," Bev said, greeting us again as though for the first time. "It's really nice to see you again, Monique."

"You, too. I don't think you got the best impression of me this afternoon."

"You were overwhelmed. It could happen to anyone."

I smiled. "Thanks."

"Well, come on in," Cole said. "Can I get you something to drink?"

"Sure," I said. "White wine?"

"Oh," she said. "I don't know if we have that."

"We do. We do," Bev insisted. "There's some downstairs." She whispered something to Cole that I couldn't hear.

"Is that stuff still good?" Cole asked.

"Does it go bad?" Bev asked. Then she turned to us. "Does white wine go bad?"

"I don't have to have it. Please, don't go to any trouble."

"It's really no trouble." Cole left the room, presumably to fetch the potentially bad wine. This didn't bode well.

"No, really," I insisted. "Anything's fine. Red. Beer. Whatever. I'm easy."

Jerome smiled, likely at the last two words.

"It's just that, well," Bev said, "this is a non-drinking home."

"O-oh," I said, suddenly aware that I'd made yet another faux pas. "Well, that's cool. I'm fine with juice."

"We've got herbal tea, pomegranate juice, club soda, lemonade…" Cole was listing off on her fingers. It suddenly felt as though they had a thousand options and I'd chosen to make things very complicated earlier.

"I actually wouldn't mind a glass of that white wine, if you're still offering," Jerome said. Thank God for Jerome. He sure was good at smoothing over the messes I got myself into.

Bev ushered us into the living room, which doubled as a playroom. There was a little tent set up. All around it were toys. Jerome flopped the koala down next to the tent.

"It's bigger than the tent!" Aidan exclaimed. He giggled and laughed.

"Is that the same stuffed animal from earlier?" Bev asked.

Jerome nodded and said that it was.

"Didn't it get dirty?"

"Bev, these things come dirty. They're dirty before they ever leave the factory where they were made in China."

Quietly, but firmly, Bev said, "Well, then I don't want him playing with it. The last thing we need is some kind of dust allergy or toxic shock."

"He's not going to get toxic shock," Jerome said calmly.

"You should have cleared this with me first," she said. "You can't just give him stuff and make us the bad cops who yank it away later."

"When have I ever done that?" he asked, this time sounding annoyed. "I never do that."

Meanwhile, Aidan was busy talking to the koala and fake feeding it a slice of pizza made of plastic. The koala's lifeless eyes struck me as creepy. I realized it was the first time I'd actually looked at the bear.

I sat down and tried to seem comfortable, though I wasn't. Jerome sat down next to me, and put his hand out, palm up. I smiled at him and took his hand. He squeezed mine as though to let me know that it was going to be okay. It occurred to me that the reason this felt so funny and foreign—aside from the fact that Jerome and I hadn't even been out on a date yet—was that I'd never, in my entire adult life, dated any guy long enough to meet his family. And here we were, not even technically dating yet, and already I was getting a glimpse into Jerome's world. This was where he spent Thanksgiving and Christmas and most weekends.

Even though I was cold, a feeling of warmth washed over me as I gained some perspective. This was his big secret at work. These were the people he worked hard for at a job he didn't exactly love. With that in mind, I took a deep breath and tried to get it together. Silly first impressions could turn into cute stories later on.

Cole came in with two wine glasses, filled two-thirds with white wine. There was a yellowy tint to the wine, but it could have been a Riesling, I thought, or a Gewürztraminer. She passed us each a glass. The night was looking up.

We clinked with each other and each took a sip.

I have never fought so hard to keep something in my mouth. My natural inclination was to spit it everywhere but I could see the wet cloud of wine droplets in my mind's eye and did everything in my power to keep it in my mouth. I looked at Jerome, who looked like he had taken half a lemon into his mouth. Both of us put our glasses down simultaneously. He took me by the hand and we ran to the kitchen sink where we spat it out.

Aidan came running after us. "What's going on?" he wanted to know.

Cole, looking up from where she was pouring red pomegranate juice, asked, "What's the matter?"

We started to laugh. First just me and Jerome were laughing but, once they understood what had happened, Bev and Cole joined in and Aidan, too.

"What the *H* was that?" Jerome asked.

"What? It was from our wedding reception. It was good stuff. Pricey, anyway."

Jerome shook his head. "You got married ten years ago."

"So?"

"So white wine doesn't keep that long. That stuff is vinegar," he said pointing at the opened bottle.

"White wine doesn't keep?" Cole asked, incredulous.

Jerome and I both shook our heads. Cole turned to Bev. "Did you know that?"

"No idea," she said, still giggling. "Sorry, you two."

"Oh my God, your faces," cried Cole, reliving the incident over again. "You shoulda...seen your faces." She took quick breaths between bursts of laughter.

"This time I really mean it," I said. "I'm fine with juice."

They all laughed again, including Aidan.

"Juice for everyone," announced Bev, like she was buying a round at a bar.

"I'll drink to that," Jerome said, taking a glass of juice then sipping it. "Mmm," he said. "Delicious."

* * * *

Dinner went much better than the first part of the visit. Bev had made a lentil loaf for the adults and macaroni for Aidan, who had apparently put his foot down over legumes one day and hadn't touched lentils since.

"This is great," I said, trying my best to make up for any previous awkwardness. "Really delicious."

"Thanks," Bev said. "So, tell us, because we're dying to know..."

"Yes?"

"Did you have any idea about Jerome's crush?"

"Bev," Jerome said, shaking his head. "Not now. Not here. Not in front of... You know..." He gestured at Aidan, who didn't seem to be paying the adults any attention. He was engrossed in his world of dinosaur figurines and macaroni.

"What?" Bev said. "I'm dying to know."

Cole agreed, "Tell us everything. We've only heard it from his side."

"I'm curious about that," I said.

Jerome put his elbows on the table, opened his palms and hid his face. "Oh man," he said. "What was I thinking bringing Monique over to you two?"

"I for one think it's the best idea you've had in ages," Cole said, slapping his back in a cordial way. The camaraderie between them was palpable.

"Can you at least wait until we've been out a few times before you start ganging up on me?" he pleaded.

There was such ease between the three of them. It felt like being in the midst of a perfect happy family. In some ways, it reminded me of the way I grew up, with my mom and my 'Aunt' Linda, who was really my mom's best friend, and her older kids. And Grandma, downstairs in her own suite where I was always welcome. It wasn't a conventional family, but it was perfect. It suited us all. Mom and Linda weren't lovers—that I was aware of—but they had a kind of partnership that superseded everything. To this day they are neighbors and close friends.

After dinner, Jerome and I cleared the table and did the dishes together.

"Thank you for coming with me," he said. "It's really nice having you here."

"My pleasure. Thanks for introducing me to your family."

"It's not too much too soon?"

"Not at all."

"So you'll still go on a date with me?"

"Jerome." I was taken aback by his shyness. "Of course I will."

He smiled, and I nearly crumbled as my knees became wobbly and threatened to give.

"I can't wait," I said. A couple of seconds later, I wondered out loud, "When are we going on this big date?"

"How about tonight?"

"We just had dinner."

He leaned in and whispered, "I know a place where we can get some beef short ribs. They have an excellent wine list."

"It's a deal," I whispered back. It wasn't that I hadn't been having a nice time on juice and vegan food, but I was definitely turned on by the thought of beef and wine. I had started to think that between the community garden and this dinner that Jerome was vegan.

"In about twenty minutes or so we can take off," he whispered.

"Sure."

When the dishes were done, Jerome asked Bev, "Is it time to reward the Grade One kid with the best report card of his life?"

Aidan looked up from where he had been quietly drawing. "Yeah!"

Bev looked at Jerome and nodded. "It's time."

"Now, Aidan, your moms and I don't want you to get the impression that you'll always get gifts when you get a great report card because doing well in school is its own reward..." He sounded like he was giving one of his talks at the office.

Cole looked in my direction, smiled and rolled her eyes as she gently mocked Jerome by imitating his businesslike posture and gestures.

Jerome continued, "But we all agreed that since you got a perfect report card, you're big enough to have your very own bicycle."

"I am?" Aidan shouted. "I am!"

"You are." Bev hugged him first, then Cole and Jerome. He skipped me, which I thought was fair enough, since we'd only just met.

Jerome and Bev said, "Come on."

Then we all went to the backyard where, out on the patio, the blue bike was set up.

"It's too late for us to take it for a spin right now, since it's dark," Jerome said with a rational tone that quickly disappeared, "but hop on and let's see if we got the right size for you."

Aidan's eyes were huge as he beheld his very first vehicle. He jumped on, and it looked like the pedals were the right height. "Yay!" he shouted.

"We've got training wheels for you," Cole said. "I can put those on tomorrow."

"We could do it now," Jerome said, suddenly sounding an awful lot like an excited boy himself.

"Here we go," Bev said. "I knew we couldn't just give it to him tonight. I hope you two don't have plans," she said to me.

*Actually, we do*, I thought, but I'd never have said it.

"Let me just get those wheels on for you, Aidan."

Cole and Jerome set to work unwrapping the training wheels. Cole went to the shed then returned with a light and a screwdriver. They set up a makeshift workshop and assembled the whole shebang while Aidan looked on.

I was freezing cold, but determined not to draw attention to it.

"Come inside," Bev said.

"I thought you'd never ask," I replied, following her in.

"You must be cold," she observed.

I shrugged. "A little."

Inside, she offered me a sweater, but I reminded her about the perfume. Maybe I should have just taken it without saying anything and let her deal with it later. I could definitely have used a sweater, but it felt wrong to not remind her. Besides, she offered herbal tea, which I eagerly accepted.

"They'll be at it for a while, I'm sure," she said, looking out of the window at Aidan, who was now wearing his helmet, and Cole and Jerome, who were heading out to the back alley. She put on the kettle and sat down. I followed her to the table.

"Aidan is really cute," I said.

"Thanks." She beamed like all proud parents do. "We love him."

She poured boiling water into a mug with a tea bag. I looked at the clock that hung on the wall behind her. It wasn't yet eight. There was plenty of time.

Bev told me all about Jerome when he was younger, how she had worried that she had scarred his relationship toward all women, how he'd been such a gentleman when she'd told him she was bi-curious and, again, when she knew she was definitely a lesbian.

"Our relationship is much deeper than that," she said. "We were friends all throughout high school, then we dated and now we're closer than ever."

It was sweet, but I wondered where I fit into everything. They had such a complete story. The horrible feeling I'd had earlier in the day when I'd thought they were a couple was awful, like a bout of food poisoning. A wave of insecurity came flooding over me. I had barely been able to commit to a shade of lipstick in my early twenties. Jerome and Bev had somehow managed to have a long-term relationship that had evolved into a friendship and now they had this beautiful chosen family complete with a child. I couldn't help but think that although I had my friends—and I'd have done anything for them and they for me—I had somehow missed out on this fundamental development in life. I didn't want to tell Jerome that I'd never had a serious relationship. He seemed so emotionally mature to me.

# Chapter Eight

When we got to Jerome's favorite haunt, Stephano's, the guy who held the door open for me turned out to be none other than Stephano himself. Walking in, I didn't know what to expect. From the outside, it was pretty plain and I had never heard of it before. It was in a neighborhood I barely knew and the sign out front looked like it had been the same for the last thirty years, which made me wonder. If it had been around for three decades, why was it never written up in any food magazines?

Inside, it was cozy and on the dark side, with tiny wooden tables, each lit with a red candle in a chianti bottle. It was like stepping into the 1970s. And it was so well-preserved that it was retro, so unpretentious that it could be trendy. There was a sizable crowd in the place, but not of the fashionable variety. This place was not the kind of place I'd pictured myself on a date with the fabulously handsome and well-dressed Jerome, but from what I'd learned about him earlier, I knew that this was the kind of place he actually liked.

A large man with a big belly waved in our direction.

"Jerome!" He smiled.

"Giovanni!"

He gestured for us to go over to the table in the corner. As though Jerome could read my confused mind, he said, "Isn't this place great? Giovanni and his brother Stephano have run it for years."

"It's really cute," I said, grabbing hold of my chair.

"Wait, wait, wait," I heard, as the large man made his way over to us. "I cannot let a beautiful woman pull out her own chair. Jerome! What's the matter with you?"

"Right, right," he capitulated like a boy who'd been caught sneaking a cookie. "I'm sorry," he said to me.

"It's fine." I smiled. *Who pulls out chairs for women these days?* No guy I'd ever dated, that was for sure. I hadn't even noticed.

Giovanni, however, made me feel special and attended to. While he pushed my seat in beneath my descending hips, I said, "A girl could get used to this."

Giovanni looked at Jerome. "You see?"

"Lesson learned," he said, nodding.

"So what kind of wine will you be having tonight? How about two glasses of shiraz? I've been drinking it all evening. Can you tell? It's very good."

"Sure," Jerome said after looking to me for clues.

I was nodding. How could anyone turn down something Giovanni suggested? The man was incredibly charming.

"Excellent choice," he said, as though he'd forgotten that it was really his choice. He left.

I shook my head. "That guy is awesome."

"Isn't he? You should meet his brother. He's a character, too."

Giovanni returned with a tray that had two small glasses of red wine on it. The glasses themselves were like souvenirs from *The Godfather*. I had become so accustomed to the large trendy glasses on high stems, I'd forgotten that wine glasses also came in this size. It was adorable.

"For the lady." He put the glass down in front of me. "For my good friend," he said as he put Jerome's glass down. "It's been, what, fifteen years now you've been coming here?"

"About that," Jerome said.

"And first time with a beautiful lady. Enjoy your wine. I'll bring over some bread and menus."

"Bread, sure. But no need for menus. I told Monique all about your antipasto, and shrimp scaloppini."

"Monique? A beautiful name for a beautiful woman." He took my hand and lifted it up. Then he bowed down and kissed the back of it. He looked in my eyes the whole time. It felt a little goofy to me. I'd never had anyone do that before and Giovanni was likely in his seventies.

He turned to Jerome and said, "No ring." With a wink, he was off.

"He's fantastic," I said. "What a charmer."

"He gets away with what he can when his wife's not around. He's a big flirt."

"I had no idea places like this existed anymore."

"Yeah, it's pretty out of the way."

"It's like a time capsule."

"Wait until you taste the food."

I was salivating by then. The aromas in the air were enough to make my body forget all about the dinner we'd had earlier. My tummy rumbled in anticipation. The wine tasted delicious and the best part of all of it was getting to see more of Jerome. I liked the way he joked around with Giovanni and really liked the idea that he'd been a regular for so long.

Every other guy I'd ever gone out with had taken me to places with blonde supermodel waitresses. This place... This was stylish.

When the food came, I was more convinced than ever that this place was the city's best-kept secret. Each bite was tastier than the last. Jerome really knew his food. Was there anything hotter than a man who knew what to eat?

Maybe one thing...

"One of these days, I'm going to cook for you," he said.

And that was when I nearly lost it.

"Yes, please," I said. No guy had done that before. It made me wonder who I'd been dating all these years. They'd had other virtues, I supposed, but it was easy to see how Jerome stood apart from the crowd.

As the evening continued, Giovanni kept the wine coming and Jerome let down his guard more and more. By the time we were on our third glass—small glasses—he was telling me all about his childhood dreams and how serious he was about fulfilling his fantasy of being a cross between Giovanni and Jamie Oliver.

"Picture it," he said. "An organic urban community garden where young people volunteer to grow produce. It gets their minds off drugs and all that boola-boola that teens get up to."

"Pretty cool," I said. I had to hand it to him. Doing good for the community was a hell of a lot more than most people around here aspired to.

"And attached to that, a little organic eatery where I serve up my sandwiches along with salads and soups. We use all the ingredients from the garden. It's a vision." His eyes sparkled with passion.

He wanted to follow along in people's lives and to build a business that wasn't just about making money but about building community.

"You should see this place sometimes," he said. "It's like a family reunion in here. People keep coming back because the two brothers make them feel like they belong here, like they're part of the family."

"I get that feeling," I said. It wasn't the décor or even the food, but the people who made this place great. "There's just something about the atmosphere."

"Yeah," he said. "That's kind of what I want to create with our space in the community garden."

"You mean like a restaurant?"

"Yeah. Something really cozy that makes people feel welcome. We've got the city's support. I'm talking to a few investors, but I still need to finalize the business plan."

"Is that why you don't want to talk about it at work?"

"I don't think they'd understand. Trust me. I know those people. I went to school with those people."

He did have a point. Looking out for the good of the planet and humanity was not exactly hip at the office. Everyone was so fixated on getting ahead.

Sitting across the table from Jerome, I realized I that I'd never thought I'd date someone who wanted to run a food business. It was the furthest thing from my reality. I'd been drawn to guys with nice cars and clothes straight out of GQ magazine, guys with expensive haircuts who would take me on luxury vacations and buy me diamonds. Jerome fit part of the bill. He was as sexy as all of the guys at the office combined when he swaggered in wearing his tailored garb, but there was also a depth to him.

As I sat there listening to Jerome talk about his dream, I saw that there was one quality I had never seen before, one magnetic and absolutely irresistible quality, and that was passion. Jerome's eyes lit up about sandwiches and regular customers in the same way they did when he talked about Aidan. I could tell that the corporate world was not for him. It made sense that he'd never tried to befriend anyone in our office. He didn't relate to them.

"What do you think about the local food movement and eco-density?" he asked.

"Well, I agree that it's easy to feel cut off from food. I grew up with a hippie mom, so we grew a lot of our own produce and always had herbs and such on our windowsill."

"Tarragon," he said. "I remember when you said that at the office and I started to salivate. It's one of my favorite flavors and the way you described that turkey."

"Really?"

"Mmm. It was one of those moments when I felt like I caught a glimpse of the real you."

"What do you mean? Am I not always real?"

"You are but…" He leaned in. "It's time to level with you. You are an absolute knockout. I mean a ten. And I know I'm not the first guy who's told you that. And you're sharp as a whip. We're talking one of the smartest people I know. But from the moment I first laid eyes on you, I wanted to see behind the beautiful veneer. I wanted to see your awkward kid photos with braces and big hair or see you in sweatpants. You know. The real Monique Mackenzie."

"That's why you didn't mind the incident at the corporate function a few months back… When I choked."

"Mind? Are you kidding? That was golden. I wanted to take you and kiss you right there. I couldn't. I wouldn't. It would have been sexual harassment. But damn, did I ever want to. You were so…"

"Vulnerable?" That was how I'd experienced it.

"I was going to say real. That was you with your guard down."

"I guess I don't do much of that at the office."

"I don't blame you. You can't do it there or you'll get a knife in your back. But to see behind that wall even for just a split second. You drove me wild that night."

"So then the koala bear fiasco…"

"Was hysterical! I mean, I hoped you weren't hurt, but wow. That was a total wipeout."

"Yes, yes it was." I blushed all over again.

"You are beyond adorable when you let your guard down. Do you know that?"

When the check came, Jerome grabbed it right away, but I managed to sneak a glimpse. It was incredible to me that we'd had one of the most fun and romantic nights of my life, we'd eaten a plethora of delicious dishes and each had three — small — glasses of wine and the bill had come to less than what those trendy restaurants charge for lunch. And maybe if another guy had brought me here, I'd have thought he was thrifty, but I could tell that Jerome didn't come here to save money. He came because he loved it. And I loved that he wanted to share it with me.

"Thank you so much for bringing me here," I said.

"My pleasure."

"Bring her back again," Giovanni said as we left. "A beautiful woman with a healthy appetite is gold."

\* \* \* \*

When our taxi pulled up to my house, I couldn't help but ask, "So, want to come in?"

"I'd love to," Jerome said.

Once inside, I offered him a seat in the living room. "Make yourself at home," I said, thinking afterwards that perhaps that was a little forward. I didn't want him to think I wanted him to move in, or that I was already picturing him living here in my mind's eye. But the truth was, I did like the sight of him in my place. I could get used to seeing him on a regular basis.

After slipping off my heels, and lighting a few candles, I turned on some soft music. I offered some wine but Jerome favored sparkling water and when he said it, I realized that I felt the same way. It'd be nice to have a bit of carbonation.

I offered him a glass, and we took slow sips, looking at each other like we were the only two people on Earth.

He shook his head from side to side, like he was savoring the motion itself. "Monique Mackenzie. I cannot believe I got to spend all day with you."

I let out a muffled laugh. He had no idea how flattered I was, how much I loved to hear him say my name. I felt the same way.

With my water set down on the table, I leaned in, closed my eyes and felt his lips brush against mine. We hovered there, like we were just rubbing noses. I felt tingles all over my body and I was covered in goosebumps. It was heaven to feel this way. He took my face in his big muscular hands and held it, while he continued to tease my wanting lips. Just when I thought I couldn't take it anymore, he pulled me even closer, and our lips joined. It was like I couldn't get enough of him. I needed to kiss him so hard that he would know how I felt. I wanted my kiss to convey the gratitude I felt that he had opened up to me. I longed to show him everything through my lips.

I could feel myself getting wet, my pussy quivering at the nearness to him. It was like I'd been on a deprivation diet for years and now there was a big tub of my very favorite ice cream right in front of me and all that stood in the way was my own choice to sink the spoon into the sweetness. I'd waited so long. The journey had been wrought with challenges and now here he was, sitting on my sofa, kissing me. Here we were, two lovers who had found each other. I was not about to let him leave without showing him how I felt.

He explored me with his hands—first the delicate caress of my cheek, then the firmer grasp behind my neck, the stroke down around my shoulder and finally the slow descent to the small of my back. It was intoxicating, like I had never been touched before. Maybe I hadn't. Certainly, I'd never had so much invested before. I'd never felt so much.

"Jerome," I said, my mind suddenly flooded with thoughts, overwhelmed with emotion. "I can't believe I'm saying this, because honestly I've been fantasizing about this moment ever since the first day I laid eyes on you, but I kind of need us to slow down."

He looked at me with warmth and tenderness. "I understand," he said. "I'm feeling it, too."

"You are?"

"I'm in utter disbelief that I'm here right now. With you. On your couch. Kissing you. It's blowing my mind."

"You understand."

"Baby, I get it." He shook his head. "You know, I had the same fantasy you did."

"You dreamed about making out with yourself?" I couldn't help myself.

He laughed. "You know what I mean."

"I do."

"Let me kiss you one more time then we'll stop for the evening."

"When you put it like that, it sounds like torture," I said.

He nodded. "Delicious torture."

I leaned forward, and his lips met mine again. My eyes were closed. I took in his masculine scent and the feeling of the soft skin of his neck as I touched him. He held me close and I felt filled with elation. He pulled back first, probably out of some gentlemanly obligation. He was raised well. I found his good manners exceedingly sexy, even if I did miss his lips terribly the moment he sat back.

We stared at each other for a while, connecting silently. It was intense, passionate and totally foreign to me. Mostly, guys had been some sort of entertainment for me. I had fun with them. I enjoyed them. I didn't stare longingly into their eyes. This was definitely new territory and it was scary. I had it bad, but it seemed that I wasn't alone.

"What would you like to do now?" he asked. "It is sort of late. Maybe we should call it a night."

"I don't want to say goodbye yet."

"I don't either. Why don't you tell me something about yourself?" he asked, smiling and nodding. "Yeah," he agreed with his own idea, "tell me something that nobody else knows about you."

"Like what?"

"Like anything. Did you have a nickname when you were younger?"

"When I was a kid?"

"Or high school. Whatever."

"Well." I took a deep breath. Then I exhaled and giggled. "I can't tell you. You'll laugh."

"I won't laugh."

"You will."

"I promise."

"They called me Sam. As in Samantha from *Sex and the City*."

He looked unaffected. "See? Not laughing. I've never watched it. Don't know what it means."

"You've *never* seen *Sex and the City*?" I was incredulous. *Where have you been?*

"I'm a guy."

"I know. But still. That show is transformational. I mean, it really changed the world."

"Sounds noble."

"The world of dating, guys and girls, how girls talk to each other. All that."

"So who's Sam?"

"She's—" I started giggling again. I didn't really know how to say it. "She's...uh...the slutty one."

"Ah." He nodded. "I see. You were the slutty one, were you?"

"Well, not really. It's just that I was in a gang of Charlottes."

"Charlottes?"

"Prudes. Well, that's not true. There were four of us and we had two Charlottes and one Miranda. No Carrie."

"I don't know what any of that means," he said, looking so sweetly oblivious to the lives of girls.

"Well, one day we'll have to have a marathon."

"Sure," he said to my utter surprise. "I'm game. I want to know more about this slutty Samantha."

"I wasn't like her, of course. I was just known for being truthful and trying stuff. I've always been like that. I mean, I love my girlfriends, but they're not really like me. I've always been a bit more daring. I got a lot of stuff out of my system in college. Let's just put it that way."

"You can tell me, you know. I'm not one of those possessive guys who can't handle a woman with a history."

"You're amazing."

"Aww, shucks," he said in mock shyness. Or was it real shyness? It was cute, whatever it was. "So you and your girls, you were pretty popular."

"We ruled the school," I said. "At least we thought we did and that was really all that mattered."

"In that case, I'm glad we're meeting at this point in our lives. You probably wouldn't have noticed me then."

"Were you a nerd?"

"I wouldn't go that far. No headgear or anything, but I definitely did not talk to girls until Bev was nice enough to talk to me."

"Really? That is so cute."

"You say now." He sat up, like he was reliving a memory and had become stiff. "Back then, I doubt very much you would have found it cute."

"On you? I would have found it adorable."

"We'll have to compare yearbooks someday."

"Oh God. No."

"I bet you were a goddess even then."

I covered my face with my hair. He'd embarrassed me. "I was pretty hip in my own eyes. Not so sure my look would stand the test of time."

"I bet the boys were wild about you."

"I did okay," I said and got up to go to the kitchen. I didn't want to get into it. "Let me get us some olives."

As I took out a plate, I went over my hesitation. Here was my dream guy and he'd promised not to judge me. He'd told me I could tell him, and the truth was I wanted to. I just didn't believe it was possible to talk to guys the way I could talk to my girlfriends. The only side of guys I knew was the side that judged, that was better off not knowing. My motto with guys had tended to be that the less they knew, the better. No emotional complications. No intertwining. I mean, I'd been asked to open up plenty of times, but it had always felt weird. I had known I wasn't talking with a soulmate. I hadn't wanted to reveal too much, especially since things could so easily be turned around. Women are still told we're bad if we try things, bad if we like sex. What bullshit. What patriarchal tripe. And if I really was talking with my soulmate now, didn't he deserve to know the real me? I could have a fake relationship, or I could march in there and...

"All right, I'm going to tell you." I placed the plate of olives down in front of him.

"Okay," he said and leaned forward. His open body posture encouraged me.

"High school was hard. I got a reputation and it was a hard thing to live down."

"Tell me more," he said.

I felt like I could tell him anything. "It was brutal. The girls were so judgmental—except my friends—they stood by me like they were my bodyguards."

"What happened?"

"Just stupid teenage boys who couldn't keep their mouths shut. Small community. The usual."

"Labels are awful, aren't they?"

"So awful." I shook my head, remembering. "And kids are cruel. I mean, teenagers. I don't blame them, though. I mean, I was more advanced than most high-school girls."

"Oh?"

"Let's just say I wasn't a goody-goody. I've always had a good imagination. Healthy."

"Ooh. Now this I want to hear more about."

"I bet you do." I winked.

\* \* \* \*

We talked for hours. I felt so comfortable with Jerome. I'd never felt this connection before. Here was a guy who wanted to know me and not just because he was attracted to me, but because he was actually interested in who I was as a person. Other guys had wanted this, had tried for this, but I hadn't been ready. We must have just not had the kind of connection that Jerome and I had—instant and intense. It was like realizing that nothing I'd experienced before could prepare me for what was happening. That is the power of true love and it is scary. In less than a day, my life had changed forever and everything I'd thought I knew about men and love and myself was all gone.

One thought plagued me as the night wore on.

"What are we going to do come Monday?" I asked.

"Yeah, that." He looked perplexed. "It's been in the back of my mind too."

"I honestly think if anyone sees us together, they will know how I feel about you because it'll be written all over my face. I'm blushing just thinking about it." I felt my cheeks and sure enough they were hot.

"It does help that we're on separate floors. Should we just try not to see each other, then?"

"Sounds awful."

"I know. But…"

"Yeah, you're right. It's the best strategy. You're private and I've got a lot to lose right now."

"Want to have lunch together?"

"How is that avoiding each other?"

"We could coincidentally run into each other somewhere far from the office, like on Fir Street. Maybe Schweiber's Deli. They make good schnitzel."

"Seems dangerous."

"You seem like the kind of girl who appreciates a bit of danger." He flashed a mischievous smile.

"I am that kind of girl."

"So it's a date?"

I nodded. "I'll accidentally bump into you there around one p.m.?"

"Late lunch. Smart move."

With that, we called it a night. I walked Jerome to the front door, and he kissed me one last time, this time with his arms so tight around my waist that he lifted me off the ground.

* * * *

On Sunday morning, I woke up alone and sat up in my bed replaying the events of the day and night before. I was glad we were taking it slow but MiniMo was outraged with me. I put my hands under the covers and felt myself. I was wet with anticipation. I needed Jerome. All of him. How had I let him leave? Why had I played it out that way?

My rational mind reminded MiniMo that there had been reasons — good reasons. When there was as much of a connection as Jerome and I had had yesterday, sex wasn't the focus. But that really made no sense, since even my rational mind would never want to be in a relationship that didn't revolve around hot sex. All the fantasizing I'd done about Jerome hadn't exactly been G-rated moments with his family or my friends. I was so thrilled, thinking back, that I'd been included in his inner circle's dinner, and I was really excited about calling Kristen up later and having a gab session. Part of the fun would be gushing about him, that was sure, but my body pined for him. And, yeah, it probably was better to take a different approach with him and not get physical too soon, but the more I thought about it, the more I was unclear on how to wait. Just thinking about him made my heart want to burst wide open. Recalling the kissing, his soft strong lips, made me long for release.

I opened my bedside stand and glanced at the available selection. MiniMo needed something, and, looking at the array, I decided that it was the rabbit. A classic. I'd shared the *Sex and the City* stuff with Jerome and what I hadn't told him was that I was among the millions of women who had made the rabbit the most highly produced sex toy of all time after Charlotte had locked out the world to spend time with it.

*Come here, baby.* I took it out of its carrying case and turned it on. The batteries were low. It was no Energizer Bunny—that was for sure. So I sat up, reached farther into the drawer where I always had a stack of spare batteries of all shapes and sizes. *Click. Click. Snap.* Now it was one powerful tool.

I lay back down and closed my eyes. What would it be like the first time with Jerome? I fantasized about him taking his time, exploring my pussy with his tongue. The rabbit's ears helped to conjure the feeling. I couldn't help but feel myself and I was so slippery. I imagined Jerome's cock. I wanted to feel it in my mouth, in my pussy, everywhere. I wanted so badly to touch him, to know him in that way. I wanted him to fill me. Thinking about what he would feel like, I penetrated myself with the rabbit and it felt so good. My pussy needed it. I pumped the cock in and out, letting the fluttering ears tickle and tease me to the point of release. Thoughts of Jerome consumed me so much I was almost surprised to find myself alone after the fantasy faded. I wanted to give myself to him.

Time for coffee. I got up, put on my light pink silk robe and, with a smile on my face, went to the kitchen to make a latte. I took a pod from the cupboard, stuck it into my machine, pulled a lever and presto, a perfect cup. On my way back to bed, I took my phone from the sideboard where I'd left it the night before.

There was a text. I climbed back into bed, propped up the pillow, took a sip and checked. It was Jerome.

*You are so beautiful. Looking forward to spending more time together soon.*

He'd sent it an hour or so after he'd left. I pictured him at home, going over the date in his mind. I wondered what part of it he was thinking of. I was so curious about him.

I replied.

*It was a pleasure. Looking forward to a random encounter…on Monday. Wink wink.*

Immediately, he texted back.

*I'm still thinking about you and how sexy you are.*

I didn't want to text back right away. I had to play a little hard to get, didn't I? So I waited half an hour and texted back a smiley face. That was all he was going to get until next time. I had fallen head over heels, and I wanted to hold onto the old 'together' me for as long as I could.

# Chapter Nine

On Monday morning, I wore a button-down crisp white shirt with a lacy camisole underneath. I could be the cool office worker while at work then, on my way to Fir Street, I could undo a few buttons and voilà — sexy librarian look. Yes, this was perfect. I put my hair in a chignon bun. I could take it down for lunch and put it back up again afterwards.

When I arrived, I greeted the doorman then stepped into the elevator. Right before the door closed, a blonde woman who looked like a human incarnation of Barbie with gigantic boobs and long legs came in as well. She pushed the number six, Jerome's floor. My stomach stayed on the ground floor as the elevator climbed up.

"Do you know Jerome Fontaine?" she asked innocently, like Bambi.

"Yes," I said. "Why?"

"What's he like?"

"What do you mean?"

Just then the elevator stopped. "Never mind," she said, looking me up and down like she wouldn't have believed me anyway. "I'll figure him out."

She was like a huntress from a horrible dystopian fantasy novel. I didn't like her one bit. Who was she? And what did she want with Jerome? *My* Jerome?

My world threatened to fall apart. I had already invested so much in this relationship with Jerome, and what did I know about him really? Sure, he presented a nice enough image, but he was a man... And men cheat. That's the one thing I'd learned in my life. Never trust a man to be monogamous. I thought back to the years my nickname had been Samantha. It hadn't just happened that I'd suddenly started sleeping around. It had been a conscious choice to avoid relationships. I couldn't tell this part to Jerome just yet, but my first boyfriend had broken my heart. It had been in Grade Nine. His name was Tyler and I'd loved him more than I'd even thought was possible. I would have done anything for him and I had done a lot for him, including his homework. One day, I'd turned the corner and right there in the main hallway he'd been locking lips with Cindy Meyer, my old rival from math class. We were always competing for first place in the advanced class so it had hurt even more that I'd come in second earlier that week and I'd lost my boyfriend to her. After that, I'd always dumped guys before they could dump me. If I'd liked them and wanted to sleep with them, I'd done it. I'd discarded a lot of men through college that way.

Somehow I believed that Jerome was better than that, but the old fears haunted me.

I sat at my desk, trying my best to concentrate on work, but all I could think about was the Amazonian warrior princess. In spite of years of education and developing my intellect, in spite of years of evolution, my brain reverted to lizard-brain status. I felt threatened. I was scared. I had to know. I wasn't proud of myself, but the sooner I figured out who she was, the sooner I could actually do my job.

"I'll be back," I said to Stephen.

This time I took the stairs. There had to be something I could ask Marjorie. Anything.

I busted into the office, half expecting some sort of porn scene starring the evil temptress and my Jerome, but instead it was the usual florescent lights and heads staring at screens. The woman, I saw out of the corner of my eye, was in Jerome's office behind a closed glass door.

"Hey, Marjorie," I said. "I was just wondering if you needed anything from me regarding the Murdoch file?"

"No, Monique. I have everything," she said with intonation that suggested she was shocked that I'd ask.

"Okay, just checking," I said. "I didn't want to leave any unanswered questions." I tried to make it look like I was looking at her, but I positioned myself to take sneak peeks into Jerome's office. He was behind his desk. He looked dreamy and handsome, but consistently cool.

"Um," Marjorie continued, "I took over this file two months ago. If I had questions I would have asked them then."

*Fine.* "Just thought I'd be a team player."

"Okaa-ay," she said like she didn't believe me.

I turned on my heels. "Well, see you at the next birthday cake."

"See you."

Useless. It's true what they say that love makes you do stupid things. No way would I normally look so foolish in front of Marjorie. Now she'd know for sure that something was up. I never should have come down. I shouldn't have listened to the jealous little devil on my shoulder, but I was tormented. I had to know. I'd have to find out some other way. It was rare for Jerome to have meetings. Could she be a client? I racked my mind for possibilities. She'd been in there for half an hour. That was a lot of time.

I really needed to work on these feelings. They weren't rational and I knew it. I'd never felt like this before. I was totally unaccustomed. I'd dated guys who had sex with other girls and it had never once bothered me. I had spent so many years being cool and suddenly it occurred to me that I was entirely and completely uncool now. Jerome had my heart and he had it completely. I didn't want to share him, not even with some blonde business meeting lady. Who could she be? Probably some sort of representative from a company. Coffee, maybe. Or stationery. It killed me that I didn't know. There was no way to find out.

Back upstairs, I forced myself to shake it long enough to get some work done. I could deal with my feelings in my time off. The hours I spent here needed to be singular in focus. *Bonus, Monique*, I reminded myself. That was the name of the game.

The day crawled by at slug speed, but finally lunchtime came around. The boys all went first and by the time the first one got back, it was twelve-forty. I logged off my computer, grabbed my coat then headed downstairs.

The air was cool, yet I marched to the deli with such zeal that I worked up a bit of a sweat on the way and had to take my coat off. I got to the deli and there, like he'd promised, was Jerome.

His smile greeted me. He stood up as I walked in. "Monique Mackenzie, what are you doing here?" He winked.

"I hear they have a great schnitzel here," I said, acting innocent and coy.

"Won't you join me?"

"Sure."

We sat down. He looked at me intently. "Hi," he said.

"Hi."

"How's your day going?"

*Do I tell him?* "It's all right. You?"

"Not bad at all."

*Ask. No, don't ask. You'll seem petty and jealous. But you need to know. No, you don't.* My mind was working overtime.

"Can I ask you something?"

"Of course."

"There was a woman in your office earlier. Who is she?"

"Oh, Kandi. She's the new temp."

"Her name is Kandi?" *A porn star name? Really?*

"Yeah."

"You hired her?" I sounded possessive, like Glenn Close in *Fatal Attraction*.

"Well, HR hired her. I briefed her on her role in our department. How did you know about her?"

"We were in the elevator together."

He nodded. "Okay…"

"And then I saw her in your office when I went to ask Marjorie a question."

"Marjorie?" He looked perplexed. "I thought you didn't talk to her anymore."

"I don't, really."

"Monique." He raised an eyebrow as though he could see right through me. "Are you jealous?"

"Me?" I closed my lips together tightly. "I don't get jealous," I said once I was able to open my mouth again. I could picture my lips making a perfect horizontal line across my face.

"All right," he said. "Well, she's apparently pretty good at data entry."

"I'll bet," I said in a snide voice. *Where is this coming from? Who's speaking?*

"Women like her are not at all my type. I prefer perfect tens, the whole package." He smiled. "I like you, Monique. *You.*"

I eased up. I exhaled for the first time that entire morning. "I'm sorry. I don't know what got into me. I guess I was a little jealous. Or just confused."

"It's okay, but you really have no reason to be."

"I believe you," I said.

"Listen, you might not know this about me, but I'm naturally monogamous. I mean it. If I'm into a girl, she's all I think about. I spent the rest of the weekend thinking about you."

"Did you?" I asked.

"Yes. You are pretty much all I think about these days. Please, for the love of God, do not let any woman at the office intimidate you. It's completely beneath you, if you ask me."

"It's pretty new, this feeling," I confessed.

"Monique, you have to know by now that you are one of a kind in my books." He reached over and touched my cheek. It was a light caress, but a dead giveaway that we were more than colleagues. I blushed.

"What are you doing on Friday? I'd like to cook for you," Jerome said. This was definitely a date-lunch, and everyone seated near us knew it, I was sure.

"You're on."

Our schnitzel sandwiches came and Jerome looked positively ecstatic. He was practically salivating. It was great to see his enthusiasm for food, but I was curious as to why he wasn't digging in.

"Why are you waiting?" I asked.

He said, "I want to see your reaction. Go ahead. Take a bite."

I cut into the schnitzel and watched the juices flow forth. Taking a bite to my lips, I was hyper-aware of my audience. Jerome watched me like I was giving him a lap dance and it only encouraged me to savor the crispy fried layer and the tender meat beneath. He sure knew where to get the best food.

"I just love watching you eat," he said. "There is nothing sexier than watching you."

I licked my lips trying my best to be sultry about it. He finally took up his fork and knife then started eating, too. After a far more relaxed conversation, I was feeling the familiar heat between us. My jealousy flair-up was over. We finished our meal and headed outside together. We walked a couple of blocks together then Jerome told me that he was going to run a quick errand and that it would be better to go back separately.

Before we said goodbye, he pulled me into the entrance of an old abandoned building. There was a tiny little corner of privacy in this nook in the middle of the city. He pulled me to him and kissed me hard. I almost melted away in his arms. It was frightening to think of the level of vulnerability I had already assumed. It was like he owned me.

"I can't help myself," he said as though he needed to justify his behavior to himself. We were both out of our leagues. We kissed again. His hands were all over me. "You're driving me crazy in this sexy outfit," he said.

I smiled. "You like?"

"All I can think about is what's under here." He pulled at the fabric of my shirt, where I'd left the buttons undone, like he was peaking behind the curtains at a theater. He kissed me there and I felt like my knees could no longer hold me upright.

I stared at him and felt my eyes go wide.

"Sorry," he said. "I didn't check if you like that kind of talk."

"Oh, I like it," I purred. My heart pounded.

"Good, because I am imagining what you look like. I want to take you where you've never been and make you feel what you never thought possible."

"Oh my God, Jerome," I panted. MiniMo throbbed. My panties were instantly soaked. I felt like I was about to be whisked off on a magic carpet ride to paradise. "How do you expect me to go back to work now?"

He looked at me with longing. His flirtatious eyes told me everything. He undid one more button on my shirt, and opened it to reveal more lace. "How do you expect me to work with this outfit in my mind?"

I smiled a coquettish smile at him and batted my lashes. "What?"

"You know what, you dirty girl."

"I do?" I acted incredulous.

He looked around and made sure no one could see us in this tiny alcove. Then he cupped his hands around my breasts and fondled me. I was so turned on. "I want to explore every inch of your sexy body," he said. "I want to kiss these gorgeous tits of yours and take my time with your nipples until you beg me to stop. Then, slowly, I'm going to lick your skin everywhere, down to your sweet pussy. I want to make you come with my tongue."

I gulped. I wanted to spread my legs for him right there and take him in that moment, which was not something the old Monique even did. He brought out something totally new in me.

"Then I want to fuck you with my cock," he continued.

I felt like I would turn into a puddle in front of him.

"Mmm," was all I could manage. Staying in a standing position took all the effort I had. I supported myself by leaning back against the wall of the building.

"You're going to take it so hard you'll scream."

"Oh, Jerome, I had no idea you could talk this way," I whispered. Like seriously, no wonder he kept such a private front. What forces had been unleashed? I blushed.

"I may have been a good boy when I was younger, and I'm a good man. I'm a good dad. I'm a good corporate manager. But, Monique, you are about to discover that I can also be a very bad boy."

"I can't wait."

"Too bad," he said. "You're going to have to wait almost an entire week."

"My pussy's already so wet for you."

"I can tell," he said, curving the round of my ass with his palm.

I lifted the back of my pencil skirt just slightly. He was standing with his back to the sidewalk. My back was against the wall. He lifted my skirt and groped my ass, pressing his index finger against the wet barrier of my panties. "You're so wet," he said in a firm, nonchalant voice.

"All I can think about is your cock," I told him.

"Oh good." He smiled. "That's all I want you to think about."

Then he gave my ass a good smack and told me to go back to work, like a good girl. I could barely concentrate enough to walk down the sidewalk. As I left him, I did up my buttons and put my hair back into a ponytail that I swiveled into a bun and fastened with an elastic band. How on earth was I supposed to concentrate on work now? There was no way.

\* \* \* \*

By four o'clock, I had to take a moment to go to the office washroom. The regular women's room wasn't going to work, either. I had to take the stairs up to the eighth floor and go into the single stall. I didn't even need to use the washroom. I locked the door and leaned against the ramp and hiked my skirt up so fast. I needed release more than I'd ever needed it before. Even Sunday morning paled in comparison to this. Jerome's words ran through my mind over and over and, with each repetition, I became more and more desperate to show him what a bad girl I could be. My fingers slipped inside my pussy so easily. I'd been thinking of nothing but Jerome's cock for hours and my wetness was threatening to run down my legs. I quivered as I felt myself. What a state I was in. I whipped out my phone and, with my left hand, I texted him.

*Just so you know, you got me so worked up I had to go to the washroom to 'relieve' myself. I'm on the eighth floor, desperate for your cock.*

He texted back right away.

*Don't you dare make yourself come. You're saving yourself for me.*

I fumbled with the buttons.

*Please? (I can't think. I can't concentrate. I can't work…unless you let me come.)*

*Get back to your desk. Now. I'll be checking up on you in two minutes. You'd better be there.*

I pulled up my panties and washed my hands. After I had dried them, I discarded the paper towel into the dispenser and left the single stall room, my face flushed with heat. How desperately I needed to come. How awful to not be able to. To not be *allowed* to. Jerome was so much more forceful than I'd imagined. He'd managed to shock me. I'd had a feeling about him when I'd first seen him. My instinct had told me that he was a sex god. But the more I'd observed him, the more I'd thought that my first impression had been wrong. After this past weekend, I'd really thought I was wrong. He'd been so well behaved. But his bad boy streak was becoming blatantly clear.

I sat back down at my desk, fixed my hair a little and took a moment to apply lip gloss. Then I went back to work. At least, it appeared as though I was working. Really, I was listening for the door. That was the one drawback to facing the window. I had no idea what was going on behind me.

And there it was — the sound of the door to the hallway. It had to be him. Moments later, I felt the heat behind my chair.

"Monique." His voice was low and sexy. "Would you have a look at this file for me? It shouldn't take too much of your time."

I turned on my swivel chair, and our eyes met. I knew he could see how turned on I was. I felt naked. I even looked around to see if anyone else was paying attention to our chemistry, hoping that it wasn't completely obvious to all that I was so close to having an orgasm right in my chair.

"Sure, Jerome," I played along. "I'll have a look."

"That'd be great. You can catch me on our intranet chat if you have any questions, but it should be very straightforward."

"All right."

"I'm going to have a quick chat with Stuart," he said in a shockingly plain tone. Then, as though we were casual acquaintances, ex-colleagues, he added, "I hope you're faring well up here on the seventh floor. Nice view." He nodded and patted the back of my chair in an amicable yet totally professional way.

"Thanks," I said.

I turned back to the report that was open on my screen. After a quick glance to make sure that no one was looking, I opened the paper file that Jerome had dropped off so coolly. Inside, there was a Post-it note that said —

*Your orgasms belong to me now. You're not to touch yourself here, at home, or anywhere else. On Friday, I will make you come harder than you have ever come before.*

Aside from the Post-it, the file was empty. My pulse raced. I was more turned on than I had ever been, and it was so inappropriate to feel that way at work. That had never happened before, not even the night we'd worked late together. He took me completely by surprise. This was not what we'd agreed to. This was the opposite of ignoring me at work. I closed the file and used the hard cardboard exterior as a fan. I needed to cool off.

I was still fanning myself when Jerome walked out of Stuart's office. In a calm voice, he casually asked — loud enough for everyone near me to hear — whether I had any questions. I told him it was perfectly clear.

"Great," he said. "Well, just let me know if you need any explanation from me."

"Will do." I swallowed hard. This was going to be the toughest assignment yet.

\* \* \* \*

That night, I called Claudia to catch up. I told her everything — the most embarrassing fall of my life, followed by a panic attack that Jerome was married, followed by my public freakout and how he'd wowed everyone at Kristen's.

"I still can't believe I missed the baby shower," Claudia said.

"It's fine — just the usual stuff, except of course for Jerome, who was the hit of the party."

"I'd have loved to see that," Claudia said. "Sorry I've been so busy lately."

"It happens," I said. "I'm really happy for you that you're having so much fun with your new beau."

"I really am. So what are you going to do to kill time until Friday, if you're not masturbating?"

I laughed. Only Claudia knew me well enough to say something like that. "What do you think? I'll be daydreaming about Friday, Jerome's cock—the whole nine yards."

"Or inches."

"I'm so curious I could die," I said, thinking again of Jerome's cock.

"I know. I can tell. Want me to come lingerie shopping?"

"How did you know?"

"A true friend knows."

"Nothing I have seems right."

"That's saying a lot, my dear. You have a whole closet full."

"Not true. A few drawers. A girl's gotta have a treasure chest, no?"

"Let's meet at L'Atmosphere downtown. Drinks on me afterwards."

"Deal. See you in about an hour."

Before I left, I stared at my phone. How desperately did I want to call Jerome and tell him his rules were driving me crazy? I had never had a guy play with power like that before. I'd never been forced to withhold. It was cruel, sexy and fun. I stared at the phone. He probably wanted me to call, to beg him to give in. I wasn't going to do that. Maybe I had met my match, but so had he.

\* \* \* \*

L'Atmosphere was delightful. I had just been paid the day before so there was tons of extra cash in my account, and although I did need to earmark some for groceries and other necessities, there was something really great about making lingerie shopping my biggest priority. Besides, the gift card would take me at least part way to fabulousness. This was not just for Jerome—though I didn't doubt that he would appreciate my findings. This was for me. This was to make me feel like I was the sexiest woman on the planet. After Jerome's Post-it, I definitely knew that I was desired. And this was the first time he was going to see me naked. There was much to do. I wanted to go to the esthetician's, too. I had scheduled an appointment for later in the week.

Claudia blushed at almost everything in this store but I was right at home. Susan, the sales clerk, even knew me by name.

"What's new, Monique?"

"New guy," Claudia said. She coquettishly added in a whisper, "He's special. We're pretty sure he's The One."

"I see," Susan said. "So nothing too kinky, then?"

"What?" I was taken aback. "If he's the one then he has got to be as pervy as I am."

"We just got some corsets in from our corset maker in France. He does the most beautiful work," she said. L'Atmosphere was no mass production place. This was the Cadillac collection of goods.

"Oooh," I cooed. "Show me. Show me." I followed Susan with a spring in my step.

Claudia followed.

Susan pulled out a box that had tissue wrapped stuff inside. "When I said they just came in, I meant it." She pulled one out. "Fresh from Henri's hands."

"Oh my God," I cried. "I have to have it."

"Well, see if it fits first," Claudia said rationally. "And whether you can afford it."

"Okay, Mom," I said teasingly.

"It will be a little pricey," Susan said. "It's handmade and each one is unique. Here, let me help you."

We stepped into the dressing room, and Susan drew the velvet curtain shut. I pulled off my shirt quickly, and she turned me so I was facing the mirror. Then, she put her arms around me and fit the corset to my front. Working expertly behind me, she started to do it up. It was silky smooth and purple. There was a charcoal trim that went all around the top and down in form-fitting lines. The ties were the same charcoal color, wide and silky, so that the wearer looked gift-wrapped. I wanted to look gift-wrapped for Jerome, wanted to offer myself to him.

When Susan was finished, she checked me out in the mirror.

"Oh, Monique," she gasped. "You're stunning. It fits you perfectly, like it was made for you."

"Claudia!" I called her in. "What do you think?" I asked when she poked her head through the curtain's opening.

"Hubba hubba," she said. "I mean, if I were Jerome, I think I'd faint."

"I have to have it," I said. It was true. My mind had been made up before I'd even seen it on myself. When I looked in the mirror, even I couldn't resist myself. I don't recall anything making me look or feel sexier than this.

"Great," Susan said. "It's six hundred and fifty, but I can give you a discount of five percent since you're such a good customer."

"Six hundred and fifty?" Claudia repeated in a horrified voice. "That was what I paid in rent the whole time I was in school. Monique, that's crazy. For just one garment? Think, Monique. Think."

But I wasn't thinking. I was drooling at my own reflection and I wanted Jerome to drool, too. I knew it was going to be overwhelmingly hot for us this Friday anyway, even if I wore nothing frilly, but I wanted the encounter to be etched into my memory forever. MiniMo was in charge.

"I'll take it," I said to Susan.

"Great," Susan said. "Would you like me to help you out of it?"

"Oh my God," Claudia said. "You can't even put it on or take it off on your own?"

"I can," I insisted. "I'll be fine," I told Susan. Then I closed the curtain and tried my best to reach the bow she had tied. It was in the small of my back, the beautiful ties trailing down behind me, like two silky tails. I could get this. I could.

I couldn't. "Claudia?" I called. "Would you help me?"

She poked her head into the dressing room again, shaking her head disapprovingly. "Do you want me to come over on Friday night, too, and help you get dressed like I'm your lady's maid?"

"Um..."

"Oh my God. You do!" She gave me her most indignant look.

"I'd do it for you," I pleaded.

Claudia thought about that for a moment, and I could tell that she knew it was true because she relented. "Fine. What time do you want me to come over?"

"I love you," I said. "How about five?"

She untied me, and we carefully took the corset off and handed it to Susan. I ran my card through the machine. Susan gave us each scented sachets for our undergarment drawers. I felt like a queen walking out of the store with my beautiful hard pale pink lacquered paper bag. My purchase was wrapped in tissue paper like I'd just bought the finest crown in the land. It was fantastically opulent. I knew it was a little ridiculous, but isn't it good to be irrationally lavish sometimes?

We went for drinks and giggled like girls over the whole experience, and I told Claudia in even greater detail what had happened earlier. Reliving it gave me so much pleasure.

# Chapter Ten

By Friday, I had worked out more than any other week of my life. I'd taken more cold showers than ever before and I'd read two novels. Still, I was going out of my mind with desire. By four o'clock I couldn't sit still. I had to go.

I got onto the elevator and there were several other people on there already. We got one floor down, when the elevator doors opened and Jerome joined us. The doors closed. We looked at each other, and I immediately looked down. I couldn't handle the heat between us. He wasn't even near me. There were several bodies between us, but all I could feel was the magnetic draw to him. It was so wrong in this environment.

He whipped out his phone and in seconds my phone vibrated indicating a text message.

I checked.

*You look so sexy right now.*

What could I possibly say in return?

He didn't give me a chance. My phone vibrated again.

*Come down to my car with me. I'll drive you home.*

At the ground floor, all the suits got out and it was just Jerome and me left. The second the doors closed, we were on each other. He pulled me to him and squeezed me so hard. He pressed his lips to mine and kissed me so deeply. I went limp in his arms. I had waited patiently for so long and now, with this kiss, he showed me that he, too, had suffered.

"Monique Mackenzie," he said when he pulled back and examined me. He raised both eyebrows and nodded. "Wow."

"I hope they don't have cameras in here," I said.

He laughed. "I doubt it."

"So, you're going to take me home, are you?"

"Yes, and if you want, I can wait for you to do what you need to do then I'll take you over to my place."

"Actually, I need to meet up with Claudia briefly first. I'm going to get her to meet me at my place." I texted Claudia to let her know to come over right away.

"Well, how about I pick you up an hour after I drop you off, and in the meantime, I'll pick up some last minute ingredients for tonight's dinner."

"Are you still planning on cooking?" I asked, somewhat disappointed. I didn't care about food as long as sex was on the menu. He could serve macaroni and cheese and I'd be happy.

"Don't you want me to?"

"Jerome, I've been thinking about your note all week. Don't make me wait much longer." I sounded forceful. I added, "Please."

"You're impatient, aren't you?"

I nodded.

He opened his car door for me and I got in. Closing it behind me, he let himself in on the other side. Once we were behind closed doors, I said, "I've been consumed by thoughts of your cock. I don't know how long I can wait."

"You need to eat."

"Do I? I think I can live without food, but I can't live without you making good on your promise."

"You're going to have the best orgasm of your life before midnight tonight. But before that, you're going to eat a delicious meal. I've been marinating beef tenderloin for two whole days. It will melt on your tongue and you won't regret my including it in tonight's activities."

"It's just that..." I didn't know how to say it, so I took his hand, guided it up my skirt, pulled my panties aside and let him feel me. "I've been wet ever since you gave me that note." I had a pleading tone. It couldn't be avoided.

He explored my pussy with his finger and moaned.

"Mmm. Baby," he said. "I've been thinking about your sweet cunt all week."

What torture! He pulled his hand back and lifted his finger to his mouth. I could see my wetness on him, even in the dim light of the underground parkade.

"Mmm. You are so sweet. You taste so good."

I bit my lip and looked at him.

"I've never seen you like this," he said, pulling out of the parking spot. "I like it."

"You have definitely had an effect on me," I said.

"I see that."

"I've got a surprise of my own for you," I said. "You'll like it."

"I'm sure I will."

\* \* \* \*

By the time we pulled up to my place, Claudia was already parking her bike in my driveway. What a friend. She waved to Jerome, who waved back. It was all so innocent on the surface. Meanwhile MiniMo was in overdrive.

As we went in, I said, "You are not going to believe him." I told her about the day's encounter. "Come with me," I said taking her by the hand and dragging her into my bathroom.

I got undressed in front of her and got in the shower.

"Monique?" she asked. "Don't you want a little privacy?"

"No," I said. I was beyond that now. "I need to talk this out with you. What do I do if he doesn't fuck me right away?"

"Um… You wait," Claudia said like it was a no-brainer.

"I can't take it." I could handle a certain level of sexual frustration, but I was mad with desire. All I could think about was how good it would feel to finally be ravished by Jerome. I'd been patient for so long.

"You seriously can't wait until after dinner?"

"No," I said in that familiar pleading tone. "I'm gonna die if I don't get some relief soon. I'm going out of my mind."

"Use the shower head."

"I can't. It's against the rules."

I couldn't see, because I was already lathering up, but I could tell that Claudia was shaking her head.

"I don't know how I feel about these rules. Don't you think it's a little controlling?"

"It's hot as hell."

"Okay, so you like being tortured like this."

"More than anything."

"Just checking. In that case, what a stud."

"I know, right? He's incredible."

"Monique, I have never seen you like this."

"I've never been like this."

"It's pretty awesome to see you in love."

I poked my head around the shower curtain. "Love?"

"Well, yeah."

"You think I'm in love?"

"Um…yeah."

"I'm horny. I'm in lust."

"You can be in lust and in love at the same time, you know?"

I thought about that as I conditioned my hair. Maybe I didn't know that. Maybe that had been the biggest problem of my adult life, the entire reason I'd had a great sex life but had never had a serious boyfriend.

"All I know is I've never felt like this."

"Enjoy it, my dear."

I got out of the shower and reached for a towel fresh off the shelf. After I'd dried off, I looked at my lotions. "Hmm," I said. "Which one says 'fuck me before dinner'?" I sniffed each of them.

Claudia chose one at random. "This one, hot mamma."

I smoothed it all over myself. Grabbing her by the arm, I dragged Claudia with me to my room where the pink bag was waiting for us.

She outfitted me in the corset, and I checked myself in the mirror. I felt stunning. Sensational. I'd had my esthetician wax off all my hair. My legs were smooth, my pussy completely bare. Every inch of me was ready for sex.

I slipped into the dress I'd planned for the evening. No panties. Just nylons attached to the garter that came with the corset. I was gift-wrapped and ready.

* * * *

Jerome picked me up, and I kissed Claudia goodbye on both cheeks, like I was Cinderella leaving for the ball.

When I got in the car, though, Jerome's expression was solemn. "Listen, there's been a change of plans."

"What?"

"Aidan's in the Emergency Ward. We have to go see him," he said. "Or, well, *I* have to go. You have a choice whether you want to come or not."

"I'll come," I said. "What happened?" Just like that, MiniMo was off duty and the real me clocked in. I looked out of the window at what had previously been a dreamy evening. Now the streets seemed foreboding.

"He had a fall, apparently," Jerome put the car in drive and we were off.

"Oh no," I said. There was a scratchy feeling in the back of my mouth and I couldn't swallow. I wanted him to be okay. I needed him to be okay. And now I understood how Jerome's life was different from guys who just had to look after themselves. Looking over at him, I saw the protective part of him in full bloom. His eyes were fierce like a tiger ready to pounce, as he concentrated on getting us to the hospital as quickly as we could. The urgency about him was undeniably sexy. I read once that you can tell a lot about a man by how he treated his mother and his pets. Jerome had no pets and his mother lived far away, but I knew right then and there precisely what kind of a man Jerome was and I was in awe of him.

We arrived at the hospital, and, after checking in, we went straight to his room where Bev and Cole were already sitting with him, holding both of his hands.

"So good you're here," Bev said quietly.

Aidan looked up from his hospital bed. "Daddy?"

"I'm here, son," Jerome said.

"I slipped," he said. "I was climbing the tree and I slipped."

"You were climbing a tree? Where? At school?"

Aidan nodded.

Jerome said, "I knew that apple tree was bad news. Didn't I say so?"

"It wasn't the apple tree?"

"No?"

"It was the oak tree."

"That tree's huge."

"Yeah." He nodded like he was proud of himself. "Cindy bet me I couldn't do it, so I did it."

"You did this to impress a girl?" he asked. A smile threatened to show itself beneath the veneer of severity. Jerome was either amused or proud, I was not sure which.

Aidan shrugged.

"Well, was she impressed?" Jerome asked.

Aidan nodded. "No one's ever made it past the first limb before."

"How high did you climb?"

"I got almost all the way to the top."

"That's really high. That's where you fell from?"

He nodded.

Just then, the doctor came in. She had X-rays with her. "So, what we have here is a very lucky boy who could have broken something. He didn't. But I don't want the scrapes here to get infected, so let's clean them up before you leave."

Bev and Cole exhaled dramatically. "That's so much better than what I was expecting," Cole said quietly.

The doctor turned to go. "I'll be back in a jiffy and we'll get started."

"All right," Bev said. "Phew. Aidan, you are very lucky. No more climbing trees, though. Okay?"

"Okay, Mommy."

Jerome, who had also let out a sigh of relief, bent down to kiss Aidan's forehead. "All right, son, we're going to get going again. I'm so glad you're okay."

"No," he objected and took Jerome's hand. "I want you here."

"Aidan," Jerome pleaded. "I promised Monique."

"I need you."

The child had resolve. That was clear. He, too, was someone who knew exactly what he wanted. I knew precisely where he got that from.

"Can I have a minute?" Jerome asked all of us.

We went into the hallway and left the two men to talk. Cole and Bev were apologetic.

"You two have a date planned tonight, right?" Cole asked.

I nodded.

Bev said, "Yeah, Jerome told us. Thanks for being a good sport about this."

"Of course," I said. "Jerome was really worried."

They both smiled. Bev took my hand and squeezed it. "She's a keeper," she said to Cole, but she was looking into my eyes when she said it.

"Uh… Thanks."

On the way over, I'd secretly prayed for the kid to be fine so I could have my sex god back. But now that he really was going to be okay, I realized that it would be fine if we had to postpone. Aidan came first. I understood that. Perhaps it was that glimpse into Jerome's face when Aidan's state had been uncertain that had done it for me. I knew that he lived for something greater than himself and I saw a depth of love in him as vast as the ocean. My sex god, I realized, was so much more than a mere deity.

"We'll take care of him, no matter what either of those two say," Cole said, gesturing to the room. She must have known that Jerome's nature would dictate that he stay. She understood.

"Thanks," I said.

The door opened, and Jerome came out. "He wants me to stay while the doctor puts the bandages on."

"Too bad," Cole said. "You have a date. We got this."

"It's his first trip to Emergency." Jerome was so responsible and it made him sexier than ever.

"And his moms are here for him. Don't worry. Enjoy yourself."

"Are you sure?"

Bev insisted, "Go." She shooed him away with her hand gestures.

"Let me just say goodbye."

He went back in then came out soon after with tears in his eyes. He took my hand and together we left the hospital.

"I have to learn to let go," he said on the way back to the car. "He's got two other parents. He doesn't need me there for every little thing."

"We should visit him tomorrow. Maybe bring him some balloons."

"Great idea. I'm so glad you understand."

I took his hand, and we made our way through the fluorescent-lit hallways. We walked in silence for a bit as he absorbed the experiences. As we approached his car, he stopped me, pulled my hair aside then kissed my neck. "I'm ready to give you all my attention now."

"I'd like that," I said.

He went to open my door, but I took his face in my hands, cradling him in my palms, and told him he was a good father and a good man. Then I kissed him tenderly. I wanted him to know that I really meant what I said. He had made commitments before I came along and I understood that.

"You're my dream girl," he said.

\* \* \* \*

He opened the door to his apartment. "Welcome to my humble abode."

There was nothing humble about it. He had a gorgeous apartment that opened into a spacious living room with a big-screen TV and a couch in the center. It was a bachelor dream pad. But there was also tasteful art on the walls and it was very clean.

Once again I wondered who I'd been going home with before. I was used to a certain guy smell. Jerome's apartment didn't have that smell.

"Nice place," I said.

"Thanks. I've been here for almost a decade now. The neighbors are good and the landlord keeps the rent reasonable."

"That's nice." On top of everything else, he was friends with his neighbors, too? Was this guy for real? "Ooh," I said, heading for the window, "what a view."

"Not bad, right?"

"Beautiful!"

"Not as beautiful as you," he said. "Can I get you something to drink?"

"Sure, what do you have?"

"How about a glass of malbec?" He took a bottle he'd clearly prepared in advance. "This is a good one."

"Yes, please."

He uncorked it and said we should let it stand a bit first and give it a chance to breathe.

He put on an apron and I couldn't help but stare.

"Now that is a sexy image," I said. "A hot guy in an apron."

He laughed. "I love cooking but I don't want to get my clothes dirty."

"You know what'd be better?"

"What?"

"If you were naked beneath the apron."

"You have a bit of a one-track mind, don't you?"

"Around you, yes."

"Then I'm going to let you have a bit of an appetizer before we eat. This roast still needs some time in the oven."

He took something foil-wrapped out of the fridge. Then he put some saucepans on the stove and turned them on minimum heat.

"I'll be right back," he said.

When he returned, he was wearing nothing but the apron. Finally, I got to see his arms and legs and hints of his chest behind the red fabric, just like he was that day at the community garden. It was hard to believe how built he was. I'd almost convinced myself that I was seeing things before, that he couldn't really be that sexy. But he was so incredibly hot, I wanted to wrestle him to the ground and climb on top of him and have my way with him.

"Jerome Fontaine," I said. "Wow."

"You like what you see?"

"I sure do. Come here," I said.

He came over to where I was sitting, and I put my arms around him. He flexed his ass muscles when my hands landed there. He was strong.

"You sure are coy with this apron standing in the way."

"I'm coy?"

I nodded. "You know I want to take you in my mouth, don't you?"

His tone was serious. "I never would have guessed that you could be so forward."

"Oh, I'm forward."

"Well, far be it for me to stand in the way of a lady's desires."

I could see that behind the fabric of the apron, his cock was getting hard. I stroked the front of the fabric lightly.

He raised his eyebrows like he was still unsure that I meant what I said.

I whisked away the cover and saw the most beautiful cock I've ever laid eyes on. He was so endowed, so incredibly delicious looking that I couldn't control myself. I had to have him.

I took him into my mouth, and he grew harder. He moaned and put his hands on my shoulders. I'd waited so long for this. I wanted nothing more than to feel him get as excited as I was. My movements were slow, steady and gentle, like I was savoring something so sweet I didn't dare rush. He stood still and let me do the moving, as though to suggest to me that anything I did was welcome. I found it so hot to be in charge of his pleasure. I looked up at him to observe his face. He was looking at me like he was trying to capture the image. I was momentarily reminded of the act of filming, and I imagined Jerome with a camera. It was natural with him. I'd let him do that in the future. Right now, it felt like he was recording with the camera of his mind, which was so sensual. His cock stiffened, and I cupped his testicles in my hands, cradling them as his cock grew harder and harder. His erect cock was a thing to be admired. He was definitely porn star material, my porn star. They could sell dildos modeled on his cock, like they did with some of the really famous gay porn stars. But I wouldn't want to share this with the mass market. This cock was mine, all mine. I took him in my mouth. I moaned and the vibration must have given him another sensation because he tilted his head back, momentarily stretching. His cock was now totally perpendicular to his body, a perfect phallus.

"Mmm." He moaned. "Oh, baby."

I hummed again, and he responded with moans. He was so hard I could barely keep him in my mouth, and I picked up the speed, licking his shaft. Still, he didn't move. He let me make all the motions.

After several minutes of high intensity, he took his cock out and said, "Baby, if you keep going like that, I'm gonna come."

"I want you to. I want to feel you."

"Yeah, but I want to make you come first. That's just the kind of guy I am."

I shook my head. It was a power struggle. Part of what set Jerome apart from all other guys was that I'd met my match.

"Well, if that's what you want, I'm not gonna argue with you, baby. Where do you want me?"

"In my mouth."

"Your mouth?"

I nodded. "More than anything." It was a power thing for me. Nothing felt more powerful than bringing him to orgasm, showing him that I could and that he'd be utterly helpless if he let me take charge.

"Oh my God. You are a dirty girl, aren't you?"

"You've no idea." I gave him a sultry smile. It was time to show him exactly the kind of girl he was dealing with.

"Well, if you're sure, then I will."

"I'm your slut."

"Oooh, baby, you talk like that and I'm gonna explode."

"Mmmm, that's what I want."

I took him in my mouth again, impressed that he was the kind of respectful guy who asked first. It made me want to prove to him how badly I wanted it. I sucked hard. With my hands I massaged his balls and with my mouth I found the perfect rhythm, neither slow nor fast, but just right when he held onto my shoulder a little firmer and thrust in and out. I moaned and that probably pushed him over the edge because he gripped me hard.

"Oh, baby, here I come."

He pumped my mouth full of hot fluid. He moaned loudly and stared at me in disbelief. His cock still rested on my tongue, offering an occasional contraction. There were sweat beads on his forehead and he released the tense grip he had on my shoulders. He stepped back and his cock fell out of my mouth, limp from having been drained of its voracity.

He sat down on a chair facing me and it was as though all of the energy had drained out of him and he was now in cuddle mode, because he put his head on my chest. I could feel him breathing deeply. We were perfectly quiet together as I held him and listened to his heart rate slow down to its regular tempo. He let out a long sigh then another, sighing in my arms. I had taken him over the edge. I had given him this state he was in. I had made him dizzy. I felt so powerful and so connected to him.

After several moments, he sat back up and stared at me with eyes that told me how grateful he was.

"That," he said very slowly, "was" — he shook his head — "incredible."

I smiled. "I aim to please."

"Oh, baby."

He grinned at me and rested his head in his hands, as though he was overcome by sleepiness. "I'm not going to be able to get this image of you out of my mind, you know."

"Oh yeah?"

"Yes." He nodded. "I will be replaying that image over and over in my mind forever. You have no idea. I had no idea. You are so sexy, Monique."

"Why, thank you."

"I mean it. I have never met a girl as sexy as you. Where did you learn — ?" He paused and shook his head. "Never mind. You are one incredible woman."

"I've been looking forward to getting to know you better for quite some time now," I said.

"I can see that." He stood up and walked around the bend of the kitchen. When he came back, he had his jeans back on and was wearing his T-shirt. His muscles bulged beneath the stretchy black cotton. "You deserve the best roast of your life."

"Are you sure you're up for working right now?"

He looked incapable of doing anything, like he'd just been woken up from a coma.

"I have to," he said. "You have to know how much I appreciate you."

"And you're showing me with roast? That's so sweet."

"Baby, I'm gonna show you with everything I got."

"I like the sound of that."

He finished setting the table as I watched. And he offered me a glass of malbec with which we toasted to auspicious beginnings. When he pulled the roast out of the oven, the warm kitchen was filled with savory notes of rosemary and sage and seared beef. It looked like something right out of a cooking magazine and I was blown away. I hadn't ever experienced a guy who wooed with food. I liked the possibilities.

"Let me serve you," he said. "I've been having fun practicing plating lately."

"You sound so professional."

He shrugged. "I watch The Food Network."

"That's so awesome, Jerome."

"You think?"

"Of course! You're putting all the right moves on me, just so you know. I've never been cooked for like this."

"You haven't?" He sounded incredulous, as though the idea he had in his mind was that men offered to do everything for me all the time.

"Nope," I said.

"Well, I sure hope to keep you satisfied." He winked.

"Mmm. Sounds good to me."

"A girl like you deserves a guy who'll cook for you all the time — and do everything to make you happy."

He added a helping of salad to my plate. "All of these greens are from the community garden. I picked them myself. Just for you."

I looked at the plate he'd placed in front of me. It was definitely restaurant quality. "Wow."

"Try it."

I took a bite and I swear I fell in love right then and there. That was it. Everything up to that point had been great, amazing, marvelous. But the roast? That really did it. The potatoes were done to perfection and the demi-glaze sauce was flavorful without being overwhelming. The salad was sublime. I was in heaven.

"Oh, Jerome," I said, admittedly in a rather sexual tone.

"Now that's what I like to hear." He grinned.

"Oooh, baby…" I had fun with him. "You know how I like it."

After we'd had a good laugh at the double entendres, I told him how much it meant to me that he'd done this. I wanted to encourage him and I wanted him to know that he was special. He was in a category all on his own.

We talked about the week, how hard it had been for both of us to concentrate at work. And I asked him if he wanted to call Aidan after dinner. I offered that we could go see him that night if he wanted. Otherwise, the next day.

"You be careful," he said. "With your beauty and sweetness and your mind-blowingly sexy moves, and the fact that you care about my son, I'm gonna have to marry you."

"Is that a threat?" I asked. "Or a promise?"

"What are your thoughts on marriage?"

"Well, it's our first real date, so I don't know if we should even go there," I said, not because I was against marriage but because in all of my twenty-seven years I'd never discussed it with any guy and I was shocked and a little scared, but so flattered. I could picture myself telling our friends and family about this moment in a wedding speech and that was the scariest part of all. *Slow down, Monique,* my rational mind told me. *Go for it,* MiniMo said. I had a throbbing sensation all throughout dinner. My whole body was turned on. I looked down.

"I don't want to pressure the conversation," he said. "But I do want you to know that I'm a serious guy."

"The truth is I've never even had a serious relationship before," I finally admitted, figuring it was better to let him know the truth. "I hope you're not disappointed."

"Disappointed? I'm relieved. It means I'd be your first, in a way."

"You're already the first guy I've liked for this long."

"How long?"

"Don't make me tell you."

"Come on," he said as he winked.

"You must have known," I said. "I mean, it was so obvious."

"I didn't," he protested and he seemed sincere.

I believed him.

He persisted. "So, how long?"

"Since the tarragon." It was a tiny lie, but I wasn't prepared to admit that I'd liked him since I'd first seen him. It was only our first date. I could give him a blow job, but admit the depth of my feelings in full? No way.

"I like that," he said. "And just so you know, I don't care about your past because it made you who you are now, but I'm the kind of guy who wants all of you, if you know what I mean. I don't want to share attention. You're a gorgeous girl and I'm sure you get a lot of attention."

"I do, but not from anyone who has mattered."

"See? That's what I like to hear. I want to be your guy, if you'll let me. I'm all about loyalty and monogamy and you can trust that I will never so much as look at another woman. I haven't in the time I've been captivated by you, you know."

"I believe you," I said.

"And I know you're going to keep turning heads, because you can't help it. All the guys at the office—"

"I don't care about any of them."

"I'm just saying. You should see when you walk by."

"No," I objected. "It's not that crazy."

"It is. You're one sexy woman."

"Well, maybe so, but my heart is loyal too. It's funny, but I really do think life works in mysterious ways. I was so mischievous in my youth. I had fun with guys, for sure, but they were all pretty interchangeable to me."

"And now?"

"Well"—I took his hand across the table—"I like where this is going."

"Let me ask you this." He looked so serious.

It was bizarre to me, yet totally fulfilling.

"Do you want children of your own?"

"I haven't yet. I mean, my biological clock seems totally broken." I was shocked we were talking about this.

"Well, just so you know, I don't need to have more than Aidan. I'm not one of those guys who needs to have a set amount of kids. I'm open to more, but I don't have to have more."

"You've really thought about this."

"I'm thirty. I think about these things."

"Well, I'm twenty-seven and I really ought to, but so far... Not so much. I'm not particularly maternal, either. I mean, I have a couple of kids in my life and now Kristen's going to have one, but generally I try to avoid them."

"I feel that way about all kids except for Aidan."

"I was nervous meeting him." I figured it was best to be honest. "But I really like him. I don't know what he thinks of me just yet, but I think I can win him over."

"I know you will. He's six. It's a difficult age in some ways. I think school is both good and bad in terms of him wanting to have a *normal* family. What's *normal* these days? But explain that to a six year old," Jerome said.

"He has a lot of love in his life and that's the most important thing."

"I agree. And Bev and Cole are great parents. Actually, this whole set-up is working brilliantly for me. I never would have thought so, but it is."

"They're sweet."

"They like you."

"They do?" I was suddenly curious. "Did they say so?"

"I'm surprised you're asking me. They didn't tell you?"

"I guess a little. I mean, Bev opened up to me that night in the kitchen."

"They heard about you for a long time, you know."

I smiled. "How long?"

He grinned back. "Don't make me say it."

It was surreal to think of it, to imagine that in a parallel world, Jerome had been pining after me the way I'd been pining after him. It seemed so hard to believe.

# Chapter Eleven

When dinner was over, Jerome took me by the hand and led me to the living room. We sat on his couch for a while and he caressed my cheek and looked into my eyes, his gorgeous smile flashing itself at me. I was unable to hide my excitement. I thought about what I was wearing beneath my dress and how Claudia and Susan had looked when they'd seen me. It was as though the thought of Jerome's reaction guided my action, but he, too, had some kind of agenda. He put on some Nat King Cole. How did he know it was my favorite? He took me by the hand and pulled me into the middle of the room. We were cheek to cheek at first, but as soon as he put his right hand onto my left hip, I could tell that he knew there was something intriguing beneath my dress. He felt around, a little coy at first, as though he didn't think I'd notice. Then his left hand joined his right and he had both his hands at my waist. He ran his right hand up and down the laces of my corset.

"Is this what I think it is?"

I looked down, suddenly shy. My grin gave me away. When our eyes met again, I saw a face that looked like Christmas had come early.

"Why don't you see for yourself?" I asked.

The zipper to my dress was on my right side, and I quickly pulled it down. He helped me out of my dress. With careful motions, he pulled it over my head and for just a moment my eyesight was obscured by the opaque fabric making its way over my face. I heard Jerome moan.

His voice was deeper than ever as he said, "Monique, you are out of this world. You are off the charts hot. I mean, wow. I can't even talk."

Once the dress was on the couch, he was shaking his head in disbelief and staring at me as though he couldn't fully comprehend what he was looking at.

"You like?"

He nodded and closed his mouth that had fallen open earlier. "Oh, I like."

I smiled and put my hands on my accentuated hips. I caught a glimpse of my contours in the glass of his bookcase and, even though I could only see my own silhouette, I knew what I looked like and I felt hot.

"You're right out of my wildest fantasy."

"Oh?" I said, trying my best to sound coy and innocent. "What are you going to do about it?"

"Get down on my knees and thank God." He laughed.

"I like the part about you getting down on your knees."

He took my guidelines seriously then pulled me to him. He cradled my ass in his hands as he held my hips so close that his mouth was practically touching my pussy.

"I can't believe you had this on the whole time. If I'd known, I don't think I could have made dinner."

"Why not?" I, again, tried to sound naïve.

"Baby, you are incredible. I want to lick you and explore every inch of you and I do believe I made you a promise about providing you with the biggest orgasm of your life."

"Oh, that," I said softly. "I do seem to recall something, now that you mention it."

He explored my midriff, feeling his way up to the top of the corset where my breasts peeked out of the tight constriction. I helped to ease my nipples out of the encasing. My breasts looked huge from where I was standing, now that they rested on the top of the corset's edge. He fondled them and moaned. I, too, let out the sounds that came most naturally—utter delight and titillation. His fingers lightly touched my nipples, and the sensation threatened to drive me mad. I caught a glimpse of us in the glass of the bookshelf and I felt like I was in the best porn movie I'd ever seen.

Jerome's tongue touched my wetness, and a shock ran through my body, almost like an electric shock, but different. It was as though, with his tongue, he signaled to my body that something so thrilling was going to take place that I would never be the same again. He got a good grip, cradling my hips with his hands as he physically took control of me, moving me back and forth across his tongue. It was incredible. Oral had not been my favorite act, but perhaps because most guys flicked their tongues and were quick about it. Jerome made small circles at just the right speed. It was slow and sensual, and I was sure that if he kept going, the orgasm he promised would build up in me and I'd come all over his mouth. The idea of it was scary and thrilling simultaneously. I'd never had an orgasm from oral stimulation, nor had any guy ever made me come with penetration. The only way for me was with the use of toys. I had a whole drawer full at home, and I'd brought my trusty pocket rocket in my purse, because Jerome had been so intent on making me come. The truth was that I had been skeptical of his promise since he'd first made it.

But in that moment of being gently guided in fluid motions to feel the entire surface of his tongue with my clit, I was in so much pleasure that I was already starting to feel the build of tension inside me. My pussy juices flowed and his steady hands made for a relaxing experience. It seemed that he could keep doing this for a long time. I grasped onto his shoulders and closed my eyes. These new sensations washed over me.

My belly had butterflies. I was nervous, yet my pussy wanted more and I found myself moving with him, like we were, together, traversing over the peaks and valleys of his muscular tongue. Then, just when I thought I couldn't take the pleasure anymore, and my pussy longed to get fucked, he entered me with his tongue. It was stiff, as his hard cock had been earlier, and he fucked me like that. Again, he guided my hips expertly, as though all I had to do was be present for the sensations. He was so deep inside me that he filled me completely. The girth of his tongue was incredible. And his touch was so slow that my hard clit was stimulated the entire time. Looking down, I was utterly blown away by what I saw. His skillful motions and the way his tongue looked as it disappeared into me then, slowly, reappeared, it was too much for me to take. My pussy constricted around his tongue and the sensation was enough to make me want to come. Just then, he slipped in his index and middle fingers. It was as though he was giving me a *come hither* signal, touching the inside of my pussy in a way I'd never experienced before. It drove me over the top with excitement as I came closer to orgasm. His tongue drew tiny circles around my now fully hard clit.

"I'm so close, Jerome," I whispered.

"Good, baby. I want you to come."

"Oh, baby, I'm gonna come so hard for you," I cooed. And deep inside the tension rose. There was also another sensation that I hadn't known before and the two feelings together built and built until I nearly fell over from stimulation. I'd come so hard, I felt faint. My eyes had been closed during my orgasm and I sat down, because my knees couldn't hold me any longer.

"Oh my God," I exclaimed.

"That was hot."

"I had no idea I could do that."

"Oh, baby, I had a feeling."

"You did?"

He nodded. On his knees, he crawled to where I had flopped down on the sofa and he kissed my knees and the insides of my thighs. He made his way up my legs, kissing me all over. Finally, he kissed my pussy. "I love your pussy, Monique."

"Mmm," I stared at him, feeling totally sated.

He brought me to the bedroom and took me again and again. My stamina had never been like this before. Jerome unleashed a side of myself I hadn't known existed. I lost track of counting orgasms. I was simply aware of each delicious moment—every touch, every silky stroke of my skin. Jerome's hands were so strong and big that when he held me, it was as though he controlled me. It was what I wanted, to be taken fully, to be made love to like I'd never experienced before. We fell asleep in each other's arms.

* * * *

When I lifted my eyelids a crack, I saw that Jerome was looking at me. I wondered how long he had been watching me sleep.

"Good morning," I croaked in my husky morning voice.

"You're so beautiful when you're asleep," he said.

I hid my face in the pillow bashfully, though by now he knew very well that I was not shy. I thought back to last night and blushed at just how much I'd revealed about myself and my tastes. We were intimate now. We knew so much about each other.

"How do you take your coffee?" he asked.

I guess we didn't know stuff like that.

"Cream and sugar."

"Mmm. Creamy and sweet, just like you." He sat up.

His sex god build threatened to turn me into a lusty lady once again, but coffee seemed like the better path. I watched him get up and walk out of the room. He looked like a male model, which was how I saw him. The muscles on his back rippled as he walked. He had somehow managed to sneak his boxers back on in the middle of the night and he looked so sexy walking around in them.

I sat up in bed and fixed my hair. There was no mirror around, but I knew what I normally looked like and figured that my hair was sticking right up, like it usually did. I rubbed my eyes and scoured my teeth with my tongue.

Jerome returned with a tray that had two mugs of coffee and two small plates, each with a little croissant on it.

"Oooh," I said.

"I hope you like espresso. I made us Americanos. I don't have a regular coffee maker."

"You have excellent taste," I observed.

"The butter croissants are from the bakery down the street. They're the best in the city, in my humble opinion. Without being too presumptuous, I was hoping I'd get to serve one to you this morning."

"I'm glad I stayed," I said. "I had a feeling I would, but I didn't pack an overnight bag. I suppose I didn't want to be presumptuous, either."

"I have a toothbrush for you."

"You do?"

He nodded. "I picked one up during the week. Extra-soft bristles."

"Nice," I said about the bristles. "Jerome, you are so thoughtful and sweet."

"I aim to please when I've got a goddess in my bed."

"I like the sound of that." I took a sip of the Americano and it was delightful. "Mmm."

A bite of the croissant revealed that Jerome really knew his stuff.

"You have a great palate," I told him.

"You think?"

I nodded.

"Thanks," he said. "You know, I wanted to be a chef, but my parents pushed me to go into business. They found it hard to believe I could make it in the snobby world of high-end food."

"I think you can do anything you want."

"Thank you. It's an incredible thing to hear you say. I'm pretty happy with the way things turned out. I'm able to afford to eat anywhere I like, but there's still a part of me that wonders what it'd be like to go to culinary school and actually put my palate to the test. For real."

"What about your sandwich business? You couldn't have done that without an excellent palate."

"I suppose. But you know anyone who wants to try their hand at food retail can do it, as long as they pass city hall's inspections and yield to health codes."

"What would you do if you could do anything at all with food?"

"My dream, you mean?"

I nodded.

"All right. I've never told this to anyone before, but that dream I told you about with the community garden and the bodega sandwich shop? Remember how I said I was considering investors?"

"Yes?"

"I'm the main one. Once I get Aidan's college fund together and save up a little nest egg in case of emergency, I'm going to take the plunge and launch this thing."

"Wow. You're working on that?"

"Absolutely. My whole goal with the corporate world was to get in and get out as fast as I could. I've already got a good chunk of capital together. I had some education debts of my own to pay off before, but the sandwich business took care of that."

"Do you really make that much more in your salary than you did with the sandwiches?"

"It's steadier work. Safer." He took a bite of his croissant. "Which is why people trade their souls for it."

"It's not worth it to trade your soul for anything."

"Yeah, believe me, I'm already plotting my exit strategy."

He'd referenced it before, but it felt more decisive now. He knew exactly what he wanted. That was what made him so hot. I finally understood that in the fresh light of morning. Jerome Fontaine did what pleased him and therein lay the key to his allure.

"Yeah, I don't want to sell you on some kind of false image. You can expect big changes from me in the next few years, that's for sure."

"Exciting."

"Do you really think so?"

"Absolutely! A man who follows his passion is pretty much the epitome of sexy."

"I'm relieved to hear you say that. I was afraid you were the kind of girl who liked the corporate type. And that isn't me."

"I will miss your sexy suits if you stop wearing them, that's true. But you looked pretty incredible that day I came to see you at the garden. As far as your career… I just want you to be fulfilled."

"You really feel that way?"

"One hundred percent." I savored the croissant. This was a moment to remember. "That's what I do. I love the business world."

"That's so cool, Monique," he said. "I respect that."

"Yeah? You don't think I'm shallow or selling my soul?"

"Not if you love what you do."

"I do. I'm so excited about the bonus. I'm rocking it. Marketing is my thing."

"You're so passionate about it," he observed. "That's incredibly hot."

We finished our breakfast, and Jerome got up to take the tray back to the kitchen. "What should we do today?" I asked, following him so I could put my arms around his waist.

"I'd like to visit Aidan, maybe get balloons like you said."

"Definitely."

"And I'd like to take you on a food tour of some of my other favorite places."

"Yes!" I squealed excitedly. "How did I get so lucky?"

"What do you mean?"

"This super sexy guy is taking me on my own personal food tour so I can try all the things he likes. How delicious."

"You might be kind of overdoing it in your mind. Lots of the places I like are holes in the wall, if you know what I mean. We won't be doing the shi-shi stuff you might be used to."

"Hey now, I am a woman of diverse tastes. Don't stereotype me just because of the way I look or dress or where I work. Understand?"

"Yes, ma'am."

He took me by the shoulders and pulled me to him. In his embrace, I felt so safe and warm and happy.

"All I meant is that when I picture Monique Mackenzie out on the town, I see a glamorous goddess. It's hard to picture you at greasy little food stalls in Chinatown, but I know some secret gems around the city."

"I'm all for it," I said. "I love eating."

"Never were sexier words spoken," he said with conviction.

"Seriously?"

"Hell, yeah. Do you know how few women will admit to a love of food?"

"I suppose they're watching their weight."

"Well, let me say, I find it sexy as hell that you're a girl who loves to eat. There is nothing sexier in my eyes."

"Nothing at all?" I asked flirtatiously, smoothing my hands over his chest.

"Almost nothing."

He kissed me hard, and we would have returned to the bedroom if we hadn't made a commitment to Aidan. He led me to the bathroom by the hand then he gave me a folded designer towel from the stack in the cupboard. His bathroom was beautiful, and unusually clean for a man. When I pointed that out to him, he scolded me for stereotyping. I guess I stepped right into that.

\* \* \* \*

We showed up at Bev and Cole's place with balloons for Aidan. They led us to where he was lying, propped up on the sofa in the living room, with the giant koala next to him. He was delighted when he saw Jerome with the balloons. He really couldn't wait to show us his scrapes. He pulled up his pant leg to where he had gauze wrapped around his leg with a bandage. He said, "This is the part the doctor said could get infected."

It was clear that he enjoyed the drama and attention, so we played into it. When I was a kid, I scraped myself all the time and never went to the Emergency Room. A little hydrogen peroxide in the kitchen usually did the trick, but things seemed to have changed.

"Does it hurt?" I asked.

"Yes." He nodded, but didn't talk to me directly. "I'm not allowed to touch it."

"No, you shouldn't. That's important," Jerome said.

"You can't touch it, either," he said to me.

"I promise I won't try to," I said gently. "Are you feeling better than yesterday?"

"I don't want to talk to you," he said.

Jerome's posture stiffened. "Now, Aidan, that is not very nice and I won't have you talking to Monique like that. Do you understand?"

"I don't like her," he said to Jerome. He looked and pointed at me.

I knew he was testing boundaries—that this was what kids did—but it still hurt my feelings. Jerome took me aside to reassure me that Aidan didn't mean it. Then he went over to Aidan to have a chat. I sat down on the couch and thought about how it might have been my fault for sending off vibes that I didn't like kids. As a general rule, I'd avoided them my entire adult life. It was so strange to suddenly find myself head over heels for the father of one. How bizarre life could be. And Aidan probably knew that I wasn't much of a kid person. Kids probably have sixth senses about such things.

I hadn't been listening to the father-son conversation, but suddenly Aidan erupted into a sea of tears.

"But I don't want to," he protested. Maybe Jerome had told him to apologize.

I rummaged through my purse and found a Kleenex then passed it to him. He took it, even though I could tell he was trying to stick to his guns and show his moms and dad how much he disliked me. I also offered him a candy that had been in the bottom of my purse for a while. It was lemon flavored. I'd gotten it from a restaurant.

Aidan was trembling with his crying fit and couldn't manage to unwrap the candy. I helped him with it. He put the candy in his mouth and stopped crying. I felt like I'd learned a very cheap form of bribery, and I wasn't exactly proud of it, but I sure was glad to see the tears stop.

"Thank you, Monique," he said.

"You're welcome, Aidan."

There was something so satisfying in being the one who was able to placate the tears, even though it was a bribe. The remainder of the visit went smoothly. Bev and Cole did their best to chat with us but they were tired. They'd been up all night with Aidan and it showed. Jerome said he'd come after work but he couldn't take the day off.

There were so many aspects of childcare I had not considered, like the inconvenience of a sick day. I found myself wondering if I would ever have it in me to be a mother and that's when I caught myself in a serious conundrum. Monique Mackenzie, the epitome of bachelorette, was aware that she might not be single anymore. Jerome and Aidan played and I watched, I listened to Bev and Cole in the kitchen talking about how Cole's mom had mentioned that she wanted to spend more time with Aidan. I sat there quietly and recognized that something new was asserting itself, a deep sense of belonging, a deep connection to this place, these people, this family… And I wondered. Were they my family?

Could I fit myself into this? Could I be Jerome's serious girlfriend? Perhaps even his wife? And could I be a maternal figure to Aidan? I would need to learn to not use bribery as a form of mollification, but then again, parents talked about that kind of stuff all the time. Marjorie and Paul were constantly complaining about having to buy Xboxes and Nintendos and toys because of deals they'd made with their kids.

And from a business standpoint, I could respect a kid for using bargaining skills. Why just do what you're told when you could try to leverage something out of the deal? It made sense to me. I looked at Aidan who was reading about dinosaurs alongside Jerome. He was such a good father to Aidan, so gentle and caring.

Jerome had his arm around Aidan and with each turn of the page, they laughed like two peas in a pod. It was beautiful.

\* \* \* \*

Later, as we hustled through the cold streets of old Chinatown, Jerome took my arm and looped it in his, as though to suggest that he would guide us. I felt secure with him. Our bodies matched so well. He was the right height for me and he had the right tempo. I'd never really liked linking arms with guys because they either walked too fast or not fast enough.

"I can't wait for you to try this barbeque pork," he said. "It's out of this world."

"Mmm" — I smiled at him — "I'm looking forward to it."

"Here we are." We stopped in front of a place that had an orange awning and bright orange and white signage. When we went inside, the warmth of the place immediately enveloped me. The windows were steam-covered and the explanation was clear. There were steamers everywhere. An older woman behind the counter greeted Jerome as a regular customer, asking if he wanted the usual. Jerome directed me to one of the booths at the back. A couple of minutes later, he joined me.

"I love it here," I said. "This place has such character."

"I'm glad you think so. I come here a lot."

He took my hands in his across the Formica table in the loud diner where many conversations were going on around us that we had no hope of understanding. Our eyes met and for some reason, Jerome appeared shy and looked down.

"What is it?" I asked.

"Nothing," he said.

"You can tell me."

"No, really. It's nothing."

"Come on. You're thinking something."

"You're good," he said. "This was the exact table I sat at the first weekend after I started working at Porter & Sons."

"Yeah?" It wasn't at all clear why he would feel weird about that.

"I wrote a really long journal entry right here in this very booth."

"Uh-huh." I was confused.

"It said something to the effect that I met this girl and it all seemed so horribly tragic because there was no way I could ever go out with her because it violated my own rules, but I knew she was the one for me."

The tips of my ears tingled and my heart began to glow like the orange signage. The tables around us seemed to disappear completely, like we were floating in our very own little bubble.

"Oh, Jerome."

I got up from my bench and scooted around to the side he was sitting on. He pulled me close to him and we kissed. I doubt that anyone noticed, but if they did, they didn't say anything.

The older woman arrived with a plate of steamed buns for us. I felt like a silly schoolgirl. She looked at me and, as though she recognized my self-consciousness, she giggled. It was the perfect exchange because I needed to laugh too.

"I suppose I should be good and go back to my side of the table."

Jerome shook his head. "Stay here."

So we ate the delicious barbeque pork in soft steamed buns while we sat side by side like we were two inseparable lovers who dared not be even a couple of feet away from each other. The sweetness of the buns melted on my tongue and each bite brought me nearer to nirvana. Somehow I'd managed to go through my whole life surrounded by guys, but I'd never sat on the same side of a booth with one. I used to scoff at couples who did this. I used to think it was cheesy and stupid and that it called for attention. But as I sat there, with Jerome making me laugh about all sorts of goofy memories, I understood perfectly why this type of seating arrangement was so nice. Beneath the table, our legs were pressed together, a constant reminder of our proximity to each other. When we got up to go, we instantly linked arms again and exited the café.

# Chapter Twelve

Jerome came over to my place. I had scoured my apartment, changed the sheets, and made everything perfect for his arrival. Normally I ate out, grabbing salads and sandwiches or soup on my way home from work. It was far easier than cooking. But since Jerome was such a foodie, I'd stocked my fridge with snacks from the nearby Persian deli. I had olives, hummus, feta and an assortment of meats with crackers. There were several bottles of wine on hand. It was a deluxe spread.

When we got in the door, Jerome asked, "Do I get to see your bedroom this time?"

"I was hoping you'd ask."

He smiled.

I asked him to sit on the sofa for a moment first. Then I dashed around my bedroom lighting candles, before quickly slipping out of my street clothes and into my silky negligee. I retrieved my man. I was ready for him.

"Oh my God," he said, looking me up and down. "Thank you."

I giggled. It was flattering to be thought of as his cosmic gift, the answer to his prayers. He was definitely the answer to mine.

Taking him by the hand, I led him to the bedroom. He entered it like a peasant entered a castle, filled with wonder and delight. It was as though he had not been tainted or corrupted, like he had not been in a slew of bedrooms. This was far from casual for him. Even in my times of fun loving and frivolity, I hadn't invited guys into my bedroom. Their place, or my living room, sure, but there was something sacred about having my man here in my bedroom.

"Thank you for having me here," he said.

"You're welcome in my bedroom."

He smiled. "I'm so glad." He added, "I must have been very good in a past life or something."

"You're pretty good in this life," I said. It was true as far as I could tell.

"Maybe so, but I'm starting to think some bad thoughts right now. Looking at you in this black lace brings out my bad side."

"Oh?" I was coy. "What does it make you want to do?"

"Well, first let's pull this strap down right here." He took the shoulder strap off my right shoulder and kissed the skin beneath it. I trembled with excitement.

"Now let's do the same over here." He pulled the left side down and kissed all across my décolletage until his mouth hovered over and teased the skin of my left shoulder. "And then there are these beautiful lips here that need some attention."

He kissed me deeply and with that felt like relinquishing all control to him. Everything was his. He eased me down on my back and as my head hit the pillow, I was nestled between the softness of the mattress and his strong embrace. I brought my legs up off the floor and lay myself down, showing him my ultimate surrender. He took my offering.

"I'd like to explore what's beneath this slinky fabric," he said, teasing my nipples by fanning his outspread fingers.

The sensation filled me with my own sexual appetite and I recognized that, once again, I was starved for him. I craved everything—appetizer, main course and dessert. I could take it all in that moment. But I knew that it wouldn't happen like that. Jerome would take his time, teasing me until I begged for more.

I moaned from his touch. His weight on me made me aware of how much more physically powerful he was. He drew the lace neck of my negligee down, exposing my breasts. Then he lowered his mouth slowly around my right nipple and sucked on it like it was giving him the greatest pleasure he had ever known. My nerve endings tingled. He alternated between the two of them, worshiping at them as he took each into his mouth. My nipples were sending direct messages to my clit, encouraging the wetness there.

"Mmm," I moaned. "I need your cock so bad."

"Do you?"

I nodded pleadingly.

"Well that's too bad. Since I'm not done up here."

I whimpered.

He slipped his right hand beneath the black fabric and slowly, slowly inched toward my awaiting pussy. He explored me. I moaned again and spread my legs apart to give him access. How I longed for him to enter me with his fingers. I needed him, needed penetration. But I knew it wouldn't be so easy. Instead, he gently caressed the surface of my wetness.

It was torture to take it this slow, but the torture made me crazy with desire for him.

Jerome lifted his two wet fingers to his mouth and tasted them. He licked them the way people in commercials lick sauce off their fingers, like they're savoring each taste to the fullest. He looked in my eyes and told me how much he loved my taste, how it drove him wild with desire, then he kissed me.

"I want you so bad," I said.

"You'll have me when I'm good and ready. Right now I'm going to fondle you and you're going to take it until I say it's time for more."

I nodded and whispered yes.

He was a powerful sexual dictator. His way was the only way and I was so wet, so incredibly ready for him that it felt cruel for him to withhold.

He adjusted our positions and spread my legs wide apart, bent at the knees. Then he descended upon my pussy with his tongue. His licking was slow and methodical. He was so good at this, it totally blew my mind. His varying pressure made me feel like I was going to come just from the touch of his tongue. He moaned and the humming sensation sent wetness out of me, dripping down between my legs, around the curve of my ass. He slipped a finger into me and I gasped.

He got up and undid the top button of his jeans. "Now, baby."

I dared not tell him I was relieved for fear that he'd make me wait longer. I couldn't take any more delicious pleasure. I was sure of it.

As he pulled his jeans down, I saw that he was hard in his stretch cotton knit boxers. His cock was threatening to burst out of the material. It was quite a sight.

"You're so sexy," he said quietly.

I sat up to suggest to him that I take him in my mouth first, but he put his hand on my chest and gently but forcefully pushed me back down. He took his boxers off and his cock was fully erect. From his jeans pocket, he withdrew a condom, which he skillfully pulled on. He kneeled in front of me, and lifted my legs, holding my thighs in each of his muscular arms. Then he ran his cock over my wet pussy, not entering me but teasing me with his erection. I moaned again.

With intense eye contact, he moved my hips beneath him, sliding his cock over my wetness. Then, he skillfully slipped the tip of his cock into my desirous pussy and I watched from the pillow perspective as his cock slowly, slowly descended into me. His cock felt so good inside. My pussy stretched to accommodate his impressive girth. How I had longed for this, how wet I was.

"There, baby," he said. "You have my cock now."

"Mmm. I love your cock."

"I'm gonna fuck you now."

"Ooh. Yes."

He thrust his cock deep into me. Then, as though he just couldn't get deep enough in this angle, he flipped me over and put me on my knees. Then he grabbed onto the sides of my hips and really let me have it. He fucked me hard, and I gasped for breath. His body slapped against mine as he thrust into me. He moaned loudly. He was rock hard inside me. He wrapped his right arm around me, and with his hand, he gave my clit the stroking it needed. That was it. I was over the edge.

I bucked beneath his touch and the tension that had built ever since we'd kissed was suddenly released.

My muscles opened and closed around him and it was clear that he felt it too, because he moaned even louder and called the Lord's name. Jerome slowed his motions to nearly nil as though he could tell that all I wanted was to feel the sensations of our bodies orgasming together. I was gripping him involuntarily. His cock gave me all it had. I wanted to stay like that forever. Jerome caressed my back then massaged my shoulders. He ran his big hands over my sides and hips as well. When he finally slipped out of me, his cock was spent.

He collapsed beside me, sweaty and blissful. I curled into his embrace and felt his heart beat when I placed my head on his chest. It was heaven. We stayed like that for what seemed like hours, silent and listening only to the sound of our breathing and our hearts beating. In that moment, I knew what perfection was. I knew the feeling of perfect alignment. My life made complete and utter sense to me, in ways that it never had before. It was an unsinkable feeling of being on the right path, of being with the right man.

"Jerome," I said. "I feel so close to you right now."

"Baby, we're so in sync. I was thinking the same thing." He squeezed me and drew me closer then kissed the top of my head. It was beyond the simple pleasure of satisfying sex. It was something far deeper, far bigger. And we both knew it. Perhaps because we knew it, we didn't need to say anything.

After a while, I offered him some refreshments then I got up to go to the kitchen, grabbing my silk robe from the hook on the door.

"Monique, you are the most beautiful woman I've ever known," he said, watching me as I left.

The sight of him on my bed felt so natural and right. I smiled at him.

When I returned, he was sitting, and he had propped up the pillows so we could rest against the headboard. I had a tray with little tiny plates of goodies and two glasses of merlot. I nestled into place and set the tray down in front of us.

"This looks good," he said. "Where did you get it?"

"The Persian Deli on Seventh."

"Oh, Mehran and Nilofar's place?"

"Yes," I said, taken aback. "Do you know everything and everyone related to good food in this city?"

"I pride myself on it," he said. "Their hummus is amazing. Best ever, if you ask me."

"Truly."

I took a cracker and dipped it into the hummus then fed a bite to Jerome. He moaned.

"Damn," I said. "I love the way you eat."

"That is completely mutual." He took an olive with a toothpick and lifted it to my lips. "Come. Taste this."

I savored the olive. Its strong flavor was like a burst of energy in my mouth. The oil dispersed throughout the fleshy bites and blended perfectly with the sip of wine I took right after.

"Isn't it amazing that people have been eating these things for thousands of years? Imagine. Our ancestors would have eaten like this... If they had lived in the Mediterranean anyway."

"I never thought about it like that," I admitted.

"I always think of that when I have olives. They sustained people. Bread, olives and wine. That's how the ancient Greeks lived and they say that was the peak of civilization so you know... Not bad."

We laughed. I fed him an olive and he fed me a cracker with hummus. It was so comfortable. So fully satisfying.

"Monique?" he asked.

"Yes?"

"I'm falling in love with you."

"Oh, Jerome." I kissed him.

"That's a lie, actually. I'm already there."

I was struck silent. I stared longingly at him, taking in his perfect vulnerability. His face was so open, like his heart.

"I feel the same way," I said.

"Monique Mackenzie, I love you."

"I love you, too."

He leaned in to kiss me but stopped just shy of doing so to rub my nose with his. I wanted to be close to him and he must have sensed it and shared it, because he remained like that for some time then he pressed his lips to mine. There was a tenderness between us that made me want to melt into him, become one with him. At intervals, his cheek was against mine. Then his tongue was in my mouth and mine in his. This easy movement was dizzying. My heart swelled with a sense of having found perfection.

# Chapter Thirteen

A couple of weeks later, at the office, Stuart asked me to prepare the big presentation for the board of directors. Our department was finally going to get the recognition it deserved. I'd poured my heart into the newly assigned Harrington file and produced results. Serious results. Bonuses for all. The last step in the process was to inform our investors, the boss's bosses. Stuart asked me to come into his office.

"I'd like you to take the reins in the meeting this afternoon," he said.

"Don't you think we should both speak?"

"Honestly, Monique. You've got this one in the bag."

I wondered if he really had that much confidence in me or whether he was simply not as adept at public speaking. Presenting to the board is nerve-racking, and I hadn't thought the duty would fall on me. But I was up for the challenge. I spent the morning preparing a PowerPoint presentation and brushing up on our results. By my calculations, there was really no way they wouldn't be impressed, since the numbers reflected big profits for the company. We had done well. *I* had done well.

But when I entered the meeting, I learned—to my shock and horror—that Jerome was sitting in on it. How was I supposed to concentrate now? This was a really big deal for me. I could not afford to blow it and his presence was a wrench in my plan. Just the sight of him took me out of work mode and into hardcore erotic mode. MiniMo throbbed instantaneously. It was a primal response and entirely inappropriate for the situation. Gulp.

"Good afternoon, everyone." I tried my best to take charge, but my palms grew sweaty and the more I tried to ignore Jerome's presence, the worse it got. I thought about the blissful post-sex state we were in and I blushed. Of course, the board members probably interpreted the blushing as shyness, and some of them may have seen it as a sign of weakness. I was weak—weak in the knees. *Oh, the torture!*

"Let me start by setting up the presentation I prepared." Since Jerome was sitting closest to the door, I addressed him. "Jerome, would you mind getting the lights?"

He said, "I'd be glad to." He got up and flipped the switch. From the back of the room, he gave me two reassuring thumbs up and a nod. It was adequately co-workery to remind me that we were also professional allies. He had looked out for me in my career. I had been inspired by his. There was more to us than our carnal desires for each other. I relaxed into the awareness that he wanted me to rock this meeting as much as I did. Instead of freaking out, I tried to concentrate on the confidence he had in me. I started speaking and I didn't stop until the presentation was over and Jerome turned the lights back on again.

Around the third slide, I was comfortable and by the end, I felt like I had nailed it.

As soon as it was bright again, I asked, "Any questions?"

To my astonishment, one of the older guys from a different firm asked, "How would you like to come work for us?"

"Thanks," I said, laughing off the compliment as I was expected to do, given that my bosses were sitting right there.

Mr. Porter looked to the guy and said, "Hey now. She's ours."

If this didn't signal an additional bonus, I didn't know what did. I was ecstatic. I looked at Jerome, who was at the very back. No one could see him give me the A-okay signal by making a perfect circle with his thumb and index finger.

I floated from the meeting once it was over. Stuart patted me on the back on the way out and whispered, "Nice work. I knew it was best to put you up there."

"Thanks," I said, trying my best to contain the exuberance that had built within.

Once we were safely back upstairs, Stuart boasted to our entire department about me. He even brought out the two-hundred-dollar bottle of Scotch he kept in his office for special occasions. We all knew about this ritual, and it was an utter rarity. It hadn't happened in the time I'd been up there. He poured rounds for all of us into little plastic ounce glasses. Everyone toasted to me and to our bonuses. I was on fire.

When the toast was over, everyone sat back down and resumed work. I tried my best, I really did, but I could not concentrate. I texted Jerome.

*I need you. Meet me on the Ninth floor. I'll be in the single stall washroom.*

This was risky and I knew it. I was breaking both of our rules. Yet, all I could think about was MiniMo, the bonus, the impending promotion and how I had my man. My life was perfect and I was in sensory overload. A few months ago, if someone had asked me to rate my life on a scale of one to ten, I'd have said I was at level six. A steady six. But ever since Jerome and I had started our journey together, I'd climbed steadily upwards to where I was in this precise moment when I was through the roof with ecstasy.

I took the stairs up. It was as though I needed something to tire me out, get me back down to planet Earth so I could do my job and get through the day. The ninth floor was deserted, as usual. There were only offices on one side of the building — the other was practically abandoned. There were some storage rooms and filing cabinets, which was strange, considering that most companies would put stuff like this down in the basement. Usually the higher up, the better the view, the more prestige. But in our building, there was this strange anomaly. I snuck through the doors and disappeared into the single-stall washroom. Then I got nervous. What would I do if someone else came?

After a few minutes Jerome arrived. I pulled him into the relatively large space and locked the door behind him.

"What are you...?"

I cut him off, "I need your cock."

"Monique... We're at work," he protested. "I don't have a condom."

But I had already begun to unzip his trousers. I pulled his pants down around his ankles then his underwear. I crouched down and took his cock into my mouth. I could tell he was a little nervous at first because he wasn't instantly hard like he had been every other time my mouth had been anywhere near his cock. Still, it only took a few moments before Work Jerome was replaced by Sex God Jerome. He tilted his head back and moaned. He was perfectly hard.

"Baby, you are wild," he whispered.

"Oh yes," I said.

"I love it."

"I can't live another second without your cock in me," I purred.

"You shouldn't have to," he said.

I pulled my skirt up and revealed that I had already taken off my panties. I was soaking wet, too. I backed myself into him, feeling cradled by his entire body. His cock was hard against my pelvis. I bent down and guided him into me. He gasped when his cock entered me.

"Baby, this is so dirty," he said.

I loved what a good boy he was. I could be the one to corrupt him. "Fuck me," I said.

And he did. He pumped in and out of my wet pussy and I felt—again—that I was grounded in my body, and knew myself. This fucking was a reminder to me of who I really was—not Monique Mackenzie, advertising executive. No. I was someone with a much more primal side. Here, in Jerome's arms, with his dick burrowing deep inside me, I was Monique the femme fatale, Monique the Amazon Warrior Princess, Monique the insatiable.

"I love the way you fuck me," I whispered.

He had me firmly by the hips and he pounded me. Hard. He did not let up. His erection grew harder and harder and I fingered my clit. I began to feel the desperation for relief. Jerome was close, too. I could tell.

"Yeah, baby," I said. "I want you to fill me."

"Baby, I'm not wearing a condom," he reminded me.

"I'm on the pill," I said.

"You are?"

"Jerome, fuck me." I didn't have time for this discussion. I wanted him to make me feel like the powerful sexual creature I was in that moment. I needed it.

"Oh God," he murmured. "Oh God. Oh God."

His cock's thrusting motions felt so good inside. With one final thrust, he pushed himself into me, and I felt the contractions of his semen entering me. That was what pushed me into orgasm. I panted and gasped for air as Jerome gently squeezed them through my clothes and bra. My orgasm was upon me and it seized control. The blood drained from my head and I became dizzy as I felt the spasms in my pussy grab onto his cock. He moaned in pleasure at the sensation and he held me tight, his arms supporting my now-weak body. I turned around and, in so doing, let his dick fall out of me. He embraced me in his strong arms and kissed me tenderly.

"Monique, you are one naughty girl," he said gently. "My naughty girl. I love you."

"I love you, too," I managed even though I was short of breath and feeling lightheaded.

"I can't believe you." He shook his head. "You break all the rules, don't you?"

I shrugged and gave him my best innocent look. "Who? Me?"

He held me to him again, squeezed me so tight I felt completely safe in his arms. For just a few moments, I savored the sound of his heartbeat that connected me to my life outside of this office.

"I needed this. Bad."

"You totally wowed them down there," he said. "It was so impressive. I'm so proud of you. How are you feeling about it?"

"Much better now," I said, pulling my panties up.

He got his pants back on and we both straightened our clothes and helped each other look presentable again.

"You're incredible. You know that?"

I laughed. "I'm glad you think so. I needed you, big time."

"You can have me any time," he said.

"Now that's what I like to hear."

\* \* \* \*

Later on in the week, I was at home one night when the doorbell rang. I opened it and there was a bouquet of flowers at face level, obscuring the man behind it. When he lowered the cornucopia of various colors and blooms, I half expected to see Jerome, but instead, it was Jack, the porn blog guy.

"Uh... Hi?" I said, surprised that he would just show up at my door without calling.

"I have to thank you," he said, handing me the flowers.

I took them. "Come in," I said instinctively.

He took his shoes off at the front door and followed me inside. I went directly to the kitchen where I pulled my big glass vase down from the top cabinet and began to fill it with water.

"Seriously," he continued, "this never would have happened without you. So I need to kneel at your feet or something."

"Flowers are plenty," I said, still trying to guess at what he was getting at. "What's going on?"

"I got a girlfriend!" He practically squealed like a girl.

"Really?" I asked. "Amazing!" I gave him a hug.

"Yeah. And she's incredible. She's absolutely incredible."

"That's awesome, Jack."

"After I left here that night way back when, I did some serious thinking about what you said. It was so wrong of me to try to film you without asking and I'm really sorry. I learned my lesson. I really did."

"I'm glad," I said, half chuckling at his overwhelmed emotional state. His happiness was infectious and I found myself really enjoying his boisterous presence. "So did you delete your blog or what?"

"Not at all. I started writing how I felt and I was honest. I made a profile on a dating site and I even linked to my blog and I said I grew up with porn and I was looking for a real woman because I was ready to have my mind blown with reality, not with images."

"Neat," I said. And I supposed I found it hard to believe because I asked, "So it worked?"

He nodded. "Yes. Totally. I got a response from a girl in York who liked my posts. We started writing back and forth and eventually we sent face pictures to each other and then we decided to meet up."

"Wow. And who says romance is dead?"

"She's amazing. We've been dating for about four weeks now and I have to say, I took some pointers from you. You gave me a huge gift that night, Monique. So thank you."

"I'm so glad my advice worked. So you held back with the camera and let her make the first move?"

"Yeah, I did and get this," he said. "She asked me to film us. She's super into it. Check this out."

He whipped out his phone and showed me his blog. Sure enough there were still shots of several clips that featured the two of them. "She doesn't want to show her face or anything, but she says she finds it really hot to be filmed."

"That's cool," I said. "Proof that everyone has a soulmate somewhere."

"I'm totally in love with her," he said, his eyes sparkling.

"Right on," I said. "Well, I have some good news, too. After you left that night, I vowed to quit one-night stands. I'd been using them as a substitution for what I really wanted… No offense."

He smiled. "None taken."

"And not long afterward, the guy I was really in love with all along came into my life. So I thank you as well."

"My pleasure," he said.

We both laughed. This was pretty hilarious.

"You want a beer or something?"

"Sure," he said.

I pulled two bottles out of the fridge and opened them. We went to my living room to hang out on the couch. I saw something in Jack that I hadn't seen the last time he'd been here. I saw someone I related to, someone who had misunderstood his own priorities. It was rewarding to see how we had each come full circle and learned to hold out for what we really wanted. We had both thought it perfectly natural to use each other in the process and now we both showed a great deal of gratitude for the lessons we had taught each other. How cool was this?

"I'm so glad you came over to tell me about all this," I said.

"Hey, how could I not? I really feel like you started me on the right path."

"You make me sound downright noble."

"Well... If the shoe fits."

When our bottles were about half finished, the doorbell sounded again. I had not expected anyone that day at all.

When I answered it, it was Jerome. He was smiling and he handed me a paper bag folded at the top.

"I couldn't help myself," he said. "I was in the neighborhood so I thought I'd bring over the sandwiches I've been promising."

"Oooh," I said, taking the bag. "Come on in."

He did, but as soon as he poked his head around the corner and saw Jack, his body tensed up. "Oh, you have company."

"Hi," said Jack from the living room couch, as he waved in Jerome's direction.

"Hey, man," Jerome said in a standoffish tone. He turned to me. "I didn't realize you'd be busy. I'll come back some other time."

"No, Jerome." I immediately grasped that he had jumped to the wrong conclusion. "Stay."

"No, I've got stuff to do. I just wanted to drop off the sandwiches for you. Enjoy."

Before I knew it, he was out of the door. I wanted to run after him. "Jerome," I called from the porch, but he was already down the stairs.

"Call me when you have time," he said. The words felt heavy and loaded, and I was shocked at just how harsh an impact they had on me. By the time I shut the door, I wanted to cry.

When I returned to the living room, Jack asked, "So, was that your soulmate?"

"Yes. I don't want to talk about it. Look, I think you'd better go."

"Well, I just wanted to come by to share the news with you. You know, Molly is really cool. I told her all about you. She wants to meet you."

"Oh yeah?" I said, though I was barely paying attention anymore. I was thinking about Jerome.

"Yeah. We should double date sometime."

"Sure," I said. I would have said anything just to get him to leave so I could call Jerome before he was too far away.

Jack picked up on the urgency, downed the last few sips of his beer then put on his coat and shoes.

"It was great seeing you again, Monique."

"You too," I said, but I didn't mean it. Not really. It had been great until it was awful. But I couldn't very well say that.

\* \* \* \*

"Come back," I said when Jerome finally answered his cell phone on the eleventh ring.

"I'm already nearly home."

"Too bad. Turn around. I need to see you."

"Is *he* still there?"

"No. I sent him away. Come over."

"I'll be there in a bit."

I ended the call and hated — bitterly — the coldness of the conversation. I'd never heard him like that before. It was scary and awful and I realized just how helpless I was. I cleared the two beer bottles from the living room then put them into the recycling bin before going to the washroom to brush my teeth. It felt, suddenly, that nothing was nearly as safe and secure as I'd led myself to believe. Jerome owned my heart. If he left me, I wouldn't be whole. He would have a part of me forever.

I was as vulnerable as I had been unstoppable right after the meeting. It was as though I was on a topsy-turvy rollercoaster ride from hell. The minutes I spent waiting for Jerome to arrive seemed endless and torturous, but this time the torture was real. It was the true threat of what I least wanted. Everything was hanging by a string and the string seemed unreasonably weak.

# Chapter Fourteen

When he showed up at my door and I opened it, I didn't feel relieved to see him. His face was not the face I had come to know. It was the cold face that he used at work. Stone Jerome.

"Look," he said. "We never agreed to be exclusive. You don't owe me an explanation."

"It wasn't a date. Is that what you thought?"

"You and some dude having a great time in your living room, drinking beer... Not a date?" He looked stern. "It looked like a date to me. I bet you that guy thought it was one."

"Jerome, you're overreacting."

"Am I? I told you I'm a serious guy. I'm not one to play around. I don't do that. I'm a one-woman kind of guy."

"It wasn't a date," I repeated. "That guy is a friend."

"A friend you've never told me about."

"I didn't think to tell you. I honestly didn't know he'd come back into my life. We had this... This..." I couldn't find the words that had felt so easy to express to Jack. "We had this neat understanding."

"And he brought you flowers." His voice had a tinge of disgust in it and I felt awful that I didn't know how to convince him. But then I remembered something.

I softened my tone. "Remember when I had my koala bear freakout?"

He nodded.

"That's what this is for you. You've misunderstood something and I need a moment to explain it to you. Trust me, okay?" I kept my voice calm.

He sighed as though he recognized that I'd used his own tactic on him.

"Come in and sit down," I said, gently. I understood—perhaps for the first time—that this relationship was precious for both of us, that Jerome also felt extremely vulnerable. He was right—we hadn't had any conversation about our level of commitment to each other, and although I didn't have eyes for any other guy, he didn't know that. I hadn't told him. In fact, the last big thing I'd revealed to him was that I was on the pill. He probably had all sorts of things running through his mind.

I sat down next to him and took his hand. My man, whom I'd come to think of as possessing the ferocity of a tiger and the strength of a bear, looked afraid. It was a sight that brought me to my knees with humility. I now believed without a smidgen of doubt how much he loved me, how much this relationship mattered to him.

"Jerome," I began. "I love you and I'm not interested in anyone but you."

"Really?" he asked innocently, as though it had not occurred to him that I'd fallen as madly and deeply as he had.

"Absolutely," I said in a reassuring tone, knowing what it was like to jump to false conclusions. "From the second you and I became a possibility in my mind, I've only had eyes for you."

"Do you think of me as your boyfriend?"

"That word," I said, putting my forehead on his arm, like I was banging it against a wall. "All my life I've hated that word."

"The word boyfriend?" he asked. "Why?"

"I've never had one," I confessed quietly. "I never wanted one, until you came along."

"Really?" He tilted my head back so I was forced to make eye contact with him. "Not even in high school?"

"Especially not in high school. Are you kidding me?" I was incredulous. Had he not been listening? I was Samantha. But he didn't know the reference, and, to be perfectly accurate, even Samantha had had a couple of boyfriends in the later seasons.

"What about college?"

"Nope. Nada. Zilch."

"So you just slept around with guys?"

"Don't cheapen it." I sent him a stern glance. "It was my choice. It's not like I didn't have offers."

"So you just never wanted to commit to anyone," he stated in a way that suggested he was utterly puzzled by me.

I didn't want to defend my past and he had made it clear that I wouldn't have to. We were different people who had met at this exact juncture in our lives and I believed there was a reason behind it. Without my past, I never would have come to know what I needed and wanted in my present.

"Jerome," I said. "I need you to hold me."

He put his arm around me and pulled me to his chest. His embrace reminded me that I was safe.

Safe enough to be honest.

"I'm doing my best to understand you," he whispered. "I've never known anyone like you before. Come to think of it, every girl I've ever met has been focused on relationships."

"Yeah, I wasn't interested in being in a relationship before I met you."

He released another sigh but in the hallway mirror I noticed that his lips betrayed him by smiling. "Monique, I'm not proud of this, but I have a jealous streak. I've been told I'm possessive and I'm working on it. I really am. But I don't like sharing."

"You don't have to share me. I'm yours."

"You have no idea what it means to me to hear you say that you've never had a boyfriend. It means I'm your first."

I nodded. "It's true. I have a past and it matters a lot to me that you can accept that. But my future is with you… And only you."

He kissed me. Long and hard and passionate. It was a kiss that lasted from the hallway to the living room and led to his pulling me onto his lap. I straddled him on the sofa and put my arms around his shoulders. He held me tight and we continued to kiss like nothing else in the world mattered.

When we paused for a moment, he looked into my eyes and said, "You know… I like that you have a past. I mean, it makes me feel confident that you know what you want and what you don't. Besides, no one can be as hot as you are and not use it. That would be a tragedy."

I smiled. "That guy that was here… His name is Jack and he taught me something really important. When I tell you this story, I think you're going to like him."

"I'm skeptical. He's already etched in my mind as an intruder."

"There, there, big tiger," I teased. "You can't pounce on everyone, you know. And I do have other guy friends that I haven't gotten around to telling you about and I will be angry with you if you bite their heads off."

"Okay, okay... Tell me about Jack." He still had a hint of sneer when he said Jack's name, but he was certainly calmer now.

I kissed him again, and eased myself off his lap. "I'm getting us a couple of bottles of beer. Then I'll tell you the whole truth and nothing but the truth."

"All right."

I returned with two opened bottles. "It all began with this infomercial about the law of attraction," I said, "I had a picture of you on my iPad and I tried to visualize you in my bed."

I felt vulnerable in telling him, but he seemed to really like that part of the story because he stopped me to kiss me.

Then I told him about MiniMo.

"You've got a name for your clit?" He laughed so hard, he almost spit his beer.

I nodded.

"Monique, you are my kind of girl. I love you so much." He kissed me again.

"So anyway, MiniMo had needs and I had to comply."

"Naturally," he said, chuckling.

I had crawled back onto his lap by then and sat facing him, straddling him. He affectionately caressed my ass and brought his hand around to my front. "I'm gonna take good care of MiniMo, I promise."

"Oh, I know you will," I said. "You already are."

He cracked up again, like he remembered all over again.

"What? You don't have a name for your penis?" I asked.

"Actually, I don't."

"Well, you should."

"Oh yeah?" he laughed. "What do you suppose we call him?"

"Oh I get to name him now?" I asked, "I'm honored."

"Well, it depends. It's gotta be something awesome. Like Excalibur."

"No way. No sword names. Way too *Dungeons and Dragons*."

"Okay, you think of something."

"I will," I said, stroking his cock lightly through his jeans. "I will take the naming of your penis very seriously."

He kissed me. "Continue your story."

"So anyway, Jack came over and I was ready to have sex with him," I said, and immediately Jerome tensed up again.

"I knew it. I knew he was more than a friend."

"Listen," I said calmly. "That was when I thought you were nothing but a fantasy. It was a long time ago and it didn't happen."

He settled down again. *Note to self – this guy is very impressionable when it comes to sexual stories.* I made a pact with myself never to prick his sensitive nerves on purpose.

"I'm good. I'm good," he said, as though reassuring me that he could, in fact, handle this conversation. "Go on."

"Okay, so anyway, I thought I wanted to, but only to distract myself from the fact that I didn't have the main prize I wanted."

"Which was?"

I shook my head. How could he not know? "You!" I said, hitting his chest lightly for effect. "Silly. You! You're the one I wanted ever since the first day you came into my office."

He looked deep into my eyes, like he was deciphering my soul. He kissed me. With my kiss, I tried to communicate that I meant every word I said.

"I don't know why I find it hard to believe that Monique Mackenzie is here on my lap telling me this. I guess because I fantasized about you in the same way... Minus the noncommittal sex and the iPad photo visualization."

"Hey," I said coyly, "I'm creative."

"So you sent that guy packing?"

"Sort of. I gave Jack a long lesson on women and then I sent him packing. And he came back to tell me that what I said really helped him. He got a girlfriend and he's really happy."

"So the flowers were…friendly flowers?"

"Platonic flowers." I smiled. "By the time you knocked on the door, I had already told him all about how I found my soulmate."

"Am I your soulmate?"

The expression on his face was so sincere, so open and wonderful. Ever since that moment, it has been forever etched in my memory. I nodded.

"Yes, Jerome. You are The One."

"Monique," he said. "I love you so much. I will always love you."

I was still straddling him when he put his arms around me and stood up. I had to hold onto his shoulders in order to hang on. I wrapped my legs around him. He walked me to my bedroom like that.

"I feel so close to you right now," he said. "I need to be inside you. It's the only physical manifestation of what's in my heart right now. I'm going to make slow and passionate love to you, Monique Mackenzie. You're going to come again and again and when you're done I'm going to feed you a sandwich that will make your mouth sing."

*Oh my!* "Jerome, you can have me any way you want me."

"I want us to explore each other like no two people ever have. I want to know everything about you. I want to learn everything there is to know about your body and pleasing you. I want to study you."

His voice was so determined, so rich like the butter in the sandwich he proffered, that I wanted to drink it. I kissed him. "Take my clothes off," I said.

He tossed me onto the bed and started tearing at my shirt. My tiger. He was ferocious again. The buttons of my shirt came undone and before I knew it, my bra was off and one of my nipples was in his mouth. He was on top of me and beneath him, I felt the sensation of being taken. He was in charge and I loved it.

As he worked over my breasts with his mouth, he pawed at my jeans and managed somehow to get them off me effectively all by himself. It was very impressive. I wanted him to be in charge, wanted him to have me however he chose.

He didn't undress himself. It was as though he couldn't wait or didn't have any need for such propriety. It felt like he needed to be inside me with the kind of urgency that didn't allow for etiquette. So he only managed to get the buttons of his jeans undone and the zipper down. His pants were still around his butt and his shirt was still on when he whipped his rock hard cock out of the slit in his boxers. He held it in his right hand and skillfully, expertly, guided it to my pussy. He slid himself inside me, and I gasped at the abruptness of it. He had been so keen on taking his time earlier. This represented some far more primal drive. He was claiming me, like I was his cave woman and he'd dragged me back to the cave and had to have me. It was hot. It was insistent and so sexy. *Yes, Jerome, take me. Claim me. Have me. Own me. I'm yours.*

He thrust in and out of me and it wasn't long before he began to ejaculate, marking me as his territory. I'd read somewhere that men release more sperm after a period of separation or after they feel that another male has been a threat to them. It made perfect sense, from a primitive perspective, that he would claim me in this way. I wanted it and needed it as badly as he had.

"Oh, baby," he moaned. "Oh God."

And within moments, he collapsed on top of me, exhausted. I kissed him and curled into him.

"Oh, baby," he said, this time gently and quietly. "I don't know what got into me. I couldn't stop myself. I'm not normally like that."

"I know," I said. "I know."

"I didn't even make sure you were ready."

"You took me, caveman style," I said and smiled at him.

I explained my theory to him and he told me it made sense. He had felt overcome by some sort of urge that he could not explain. Then he promised me as much oral sex and foreplay as I wanted. It was as though his superego felt bad about his id.

I kissed him. "I love you, Jerome."

Still wearing his clothes, he held me in a big bear hug and took the corner of my blanket and wrapped it around me. He held me tight and fell asleep. He was spent.

I had a chance to run the entire scenario through my mind again and I was glad to have made it perfectly clear to him exactly how I felt.

* * * *

When he woke up, about an hour later, he was ravenous, like a bear waking up after hibernation. He wanted to make sure that his lady was satisfied.

"Mmm," he moaned. "Baby, come here."

He kissed me. Then he ran his hands up and down my still-naked body. I'd enjoyed having a bit of quiet time to listen to his breathing and to think about everything that the past few months had brought. Now, with his hands exploring me, I had to admit that I was extremely turned on. His caveman episode had ignited something primal in me as well.

He sat up and took off his shirt then stood up and stripped out of his jeans. He climbed back into bed and said, "I owe you a seriously satisfying orgasm."

"You do, do you?" I asked flirtatiously. *Sure, I'll bite.*

"Come here." He lay down with his head on my pillows and pulled me on top of him.

At first, I thought he wanted me to ride him, but he kept pulling me closer and closer toward his face. He winked and grabbed onto my hips then pulled at me until I was practically straddling his face.

In all my experiences, this was something I had not tried. "Really?" I asked.

"Please," he said. "I want to make you come harder than you ever have. I want you to let go completely."

I approached his face with my pussy with some hesitation. This was a trust thing. This was definitely a bit strange for me. But his awaiting tongue felt so good against my pussy that I was soon comfortable in this position. He teased my nipples. I clutched the headboard for support and began to rock back and forth in a way that felt so good I couldn't believe it. I had not experienced oral sex as intensely as the night at Jerome's apartment, but this rivalled that experience. I was shocked at what this position did for me. I felt powerful. I was the cavewoman to his caveman. I was claiming what was rightfully mine — his mouth. And, surprising myself, I started bucking wildly with his tongue's motions. Inside me, I had a sense that I was holding energy that needed to come out, something I absolutely had to release. It was like the ejaculate he had for me. I had not felt insecure about my place in his world — in fact, it was probably the exact opposite that had led me to feel as though I wanted to show him exactly what he could do to me.

* * * *

That weekend, Bev and Cole had a plan to take Aidan out for a bike ride and a play session in the park. Jerome said he was going to tag along and asked if I wanted to join in. It seemed like great fun. We were going to dress for the weather — it was cold. And we would bring thermoses filled with hot chocolate and hot tea. The forecast promised the first snowfall of the year and it felt like a very romantic idea to spend that magical first snow with Jerome, playing ball in the park with Aidan and the family. Although it had only been a few months since the koala bear incident, I realized I had begun to think of Bev and Cole as family. I couldn't wait to tell them about the big presentation success and I was looking forward to seeing Aidan, too.

As he was wont to do, Aidan ignored me when we first showed up at Bev and Cole's.

"Hi, Daddy," he said when he saw Jerome, but there was nothing for me.

"Hey, Aidan," Jerome said. "Wanna say hi to Monique, too? She's going to come with us to the park."

He made a face. Then he leaned in to Jerome and said quietly, "Does she have to come?"

"We're going to have so much fun, Aidan," I said.

"Really?" he asked.

"Don't believe me?" I showed him the Frisbee I had behind my back. "I used to be pretty good at this when I was young. I'll show you."

"I don't like Frisbee."

"Have you ever tried it?" Bev asked.

I was pleased that there was growing consensus around the adults to help Aidan through his jealousy. After the recent incident with Jerome, I knew where he got it from. And it was a big deal to suddenly have to share his dad with someone new. I understood his reluctance.

\* \* \* \*

At the park, there was a winding path along which the newly proficient Aidan could tear back and forth on his bike. We adults had a good time. We set up our camp at a picnic table and tossed our backpacks and everything in one pile. Bev had made finger sandwiches for everyone, which was sweet. They were just a little snack to help tide us over until dinner back at their place. Jerome had brought over a squash casserole in the morning that he had marinated and was excited about putting in the oven.

So we tossed the Frisbee back and forth in the cold, and I felt like Jerome and I were in a fall advertisement for trendy clothing. We had flushed cheeks as we ran through the crisp fall leaves. The crunchy sounds of the first frost brought on the exact type of winter I loved. I was ready to be inside more — and ready for those cozy evenings spent around the fireplace with Jerome.

What started as a flirty game between Jerome and I turned into a fun four-way toss. Each adult had a corner and we kept the Frisbee going between us for a good twenty minutes.

"I haven't seen Aidan go by on the path for a while," Cole said. "Maybe I should go look for him."

"He's fine," said Bev, shrugging it off. "He's probably just stopped to look at something."

"Yeah, but…" Cole looked worried.

Jerome called Aidan's name a couple of times really loudly, but when there was no answer. Cole slapped her forehead in frustration. Jerome ran toward a path nearby. Bev mumbled a curse then a prayer. I had no idea what to do. There were several pathways that wove in and out of the woods. We were in a highly intricate landscape of playgrounds and swings, pathways, picnic spots and fields. Thousands of people could spend their leisure time in this park on any given day. Only in that moment did it occur to us how truly large an area this really was. It would be exceedingly easy for a little boy to get lost in the maze of it all.

"We should split up," Bev suggested. "We'll cover more ground that way."

"Good idea," said Cole. "I'll go west. You wanna take east?"

The two moms had their strategy instantly. Jerome and I were clearly a little more stumped by the situation.

"Do you want to stay here in case he comes back?" Jerome asked.

"Actually, I'd rather go look for him," I said, feeling anxious. It was better to be on the move.

"Okay, I'll stay."

"I don't know why, but my senses tell me he went toward the skateboard park," I said.

"But that's where the big kids are."

"Yeah, and that's why he wants to go there."

"I don't know. I think he's on the bike trail," Jerome said.

"Maybe," I said. After all, his parents were more likely to know. "Okay, I'll check the bike path over there. The north trail."

I paced myself so that I could run without losing my breath. The path was narrow and deserted. It felt highly unlikely that he was here, but if he were, I'd find him. Terrible ideas ran through my mind. I prayed that he wasn't hurt or scared.

I covered the length of the trail but it was all for naught. Maybe the others had him, I thought. When I entered into the clearing again, I saw that Jerome and Cole had switched roles.

From across the field, I called, "No luck yet?"

"No," she cried out. She was frantic. "Jerome took the south trail. I'm freaking out."

"Don't panic," I yelled. "We'll find him."

She called his name and walked around in tiny circles. I decided to follow my intuition.

There was a concrete pathway that cut across the park to the skateboarding area and I ran the length of it. When I came to a bridge that crossed a stream to the other side, I wondered if maybe this was totally crazy. If he had gone this way, he wouldn't have ridden very far on his own. But I had to see for myself in order to rule it out. I turned around and looked in the direction I'd come. I could tell which path I had taken because it was concrete, but it was confusing and for a six year old, I imagined that this place would seem as big as the whole wide world.

I darted across the bridge and on the other side, I found a tiny little heap of a human being. It was Aidan, and he was sitting next to his bike with his head in his lap and even from far away, I could tell that he was crying.

"Aidan!" I called.

He looked up. I waved at him.

"Monique!"

"I'm coming!" I cried out.

I hurried. I had no idea I could run like that, but I also hadn't been tested with anything that mattered in a long time.

When I got close to him, he stood up and his face was red from tears. He held his arms up to me. I grabbed him and picked him up and he swung his legs around me.

He cried and hid his face in my neck.

"I got you, Aidan. It's okay."

"I got lost," he said.

"I know, sweetheart. We were all worried. But I'm here and you're okay and it's all over. It's okay. Let's go back to the others," I said.

He didn't want me to let him go. He must have been terrified.

Somehow I managed to bend down and get his bike up to a standing position so I could push it with one hand while I supported him with the other arm. He wrapped his legs around my waist and found a seat on the bulge of my hip. I never would have thought I had the strength to carry him all the way back, but somehow I found it. When we emerged from the pathway maze into the open clearing, I saw that Bev and Cole were hugging each other, each one trying to calm the other down.

"Found him!" I called.

When Aidan saw his moms, he tore off toward them running as fast as he could. He ran into their awaiting arms and got a hug so big I was sure they would squish him. Now the tears flowed openly.

"You had us so scared," Cole said.

"Don't ever take off like that again," said Bev.

"I didn't mean to. I got lost."

When I got closer, Bev and Cole hugged me, too. "Thank you. Thank you. Thank you," they alternated in saying. We were in a great big group hug when Jerome emerged from the south path.

"He's back?"

"Monique found him," Bev called.

He ran toward us and joined the group hug. "Aidan, we were worried sick."

"I'm sorry."

"It's okay. As long as you're okay, it's okay," Jerome said. His relief was palpable. That was true for all of us adults, most especially Bev and Cole.

"I thought I was going to have a heart attack," Cole said.

"That was the worst experience of my life," said Bev.

"Pizza on me," Jerome said. "Let's get out of here."

"Yay!" called Aidan, who was clearly ecstatic to be back with us. How awful it must have been out there when he didn't know where he was.

He took my hand. "I want to walk with Monique," he said.

We walked back to the car, hand in hand, in front of the others.

This was a new beginning for us. "You're a brave boy, Aidan. I would have been really scared out there," I said.

"I knew you'd find me," he said.

"Were you scared?"

"A little." He was ready to put the experience behind him. I could tell because he changed the topic. "What's your favorite kind of pizza?" he asked.

"Um… I'd have to say ham and pineapple."

"Me too!"

He called back to the gang of parents walking calmly behind us, "Monique and I are going to have ham and pineapple pizza."

I turned back to look. Jerome winked at me and flashed me a gorgeous smile. This day had turned out to mark a very special turning point for all of us.

\* \* \* \*

At the pizza parlor, Aidan wanted to sit with me. It was as though we had become best friends instantly and now there was no recollection of a time when he'd been skeptical of me. I was more than happy to turn the page on that chapter, too. There was so much for me to learn about him.

"Who's your best friend at school?" I asked.

"Chelsea," he said. Then he told me all about her, how she liked cheese sandwiches and skipping and how he beat her at Angry Birds all the time.

Bev, Cole and Jerome watched us with glee and I felt so blessed to have been granted this very special place in Aidan's heart.

As we talked, I learned something else, too. It was an internal thing. I realized I really loved Aidan, and that I could see myself spending a great deal of time with him. I understood that my life would never be the same again, that I had found my family.

When we parted ways back in Bev and Cole's driveway, Aidan hugged me without being asked to. I knew he would never have to be asked to show me affection again. We were solid now. We were buddies.

"Can we go to the park again next weekend?" he asked me.

"Uh… I'm not so sure," I said, looking for guidance from his parents.

"I don't know if I can handle it," Cole said.

Bev put her arm around her. "I hope we never have to experience that kind of excitement ever again."

"Come on, kiddo," Cole said. "Let's go inside."

"Can Monique come in?"

"What about me?" Jerome asked.

"And Daddy, too?" He looked to his moms.

"We have to go, Aidan," I said. "But we'll come see you soon."

"No!" he said. And this time he cried because we were leaving, which was a much better feeling than his earlier tears.

He relented pretty quickly and waved a pouty goodbye to us as we got into Jerome's car and pulled out of the driveway.

"Baby, I gotta hand it to you," Jerome said once we were driving off. "You were a real champion today."

"It was nothing. I'm just glad Aidan is okay. I was so worried."

"We all were. How did you know where he was?"

"It was just a feeling. I don't know. Intuition, I guess."

"Well, thank God for you and your intuition."

"You know, I realized just how much I love him today."

Jerome pulled over to the side of the road. "Do you realize what you just said?"

I looked at him, baffled.

"You said you love my son. Do you know how much that means to me?"

I smiled and nodded. "It's the truth, Jerome."

"Oh, Monique. What did I do to deserve this? I feel like I need to pinch myself to make sure I'm not dreaming. Before I met you, I seriously thought I was going to have to go it alone forever."

"You? You're way too hot to do that." I hit him playfully on the arm.

He smiled. "Seriously. You blow my mind."

"Mutual, my love. Mutual."

# Chapter Fifteen

On Monday morning, Stuart announced that the rumors were true. Our department was getting the biggest bonuses in the entire company.

"And we all know who we have to thank for that." He asked me to stand up and take a bow.

It was crazy exhilaration to be acknowledged like that. All my colleagues hooted and cheered and applauded.

"Thanks, everyone," I said. "But we did it as a team."

"A team with your great ideas," Stuart said. "Which is why they're setting up an office for you on the ninth floor and giving you a permanent team."

"What? They're what?" I was speechless.

"Yep. Congratulations, Monique. You're getting promoted. Again."

"No way."

"Way!" Stuart said in a tone that was somewhat imitative of mine.

I knew exactly what I was going to do with my bonus already and now that I had an idea that there would be a pay increase, I was really ecstatic. The old Monique Mackenzie would have gone to the spa for the works — pedicure, manicure, facial, massage, scrub — some kind of bridal package, most likely. Then the old Monique would have gone on a shopping spree and taken Claudia out for drinks and all sorts of fun stuff. And I still planned to do some of that, but I had other plans, too — plans that would grow. Investments.

I sent Jerome a playfully forceful text.

*Pick me up tonight at 7. We're celebrating.*

He replied right away with —

*Anything you say.*

\* \* \* \*

As soon as I was in Jerome's car, it started. I could barely contain my excitement. Butterflies galore.

"Let's go to Stephano's," I said.

"Dream woman." He glanced at me as he shook his head. "How did you know I was in the mood for lasagna?"

When we got there, Giovanni greeted us and he told me he was very happy to see me again.

Over wine, I told him, "Stuart confirmed our bonuses."

"All right!" he cheered. "Congratulations." He got up to kiss me over the table.

"There's more," I said, enjoying the fluttering in my belly. It was great to have this news to report and even better to have someone this wonderful to report it to.

"Wow. Okay. Continue." Jerome looked at me expectantly.

"I was promoted."

"Again? Wow! You are on a roll. You're going to own that company one day."

"Yep." I nodded. No disagreement from me. "For now, they're putting me on the ninth floor and giving me my very own office and team."

"The ninth floor?" he asked, flashing me a flirtatious grin. We were both instantly transported to our naughty tryst. I bit my lip just thinking about it, how incredible it would feel to relive that moment later.

I nodded.

Jerome continued, "That is amazing. I hadn't heard a thing about it. It's over my head now. You're officially higher in the ranks."

For a moment, I wondered if that bothered him. Secretly, I'd always hated reading women's magazines for the one reason that they planted this terrible fear in me of the male ego and its boundlessness. Ever since I'd entered the corporate world, I'd been afraid of becoming so successful that I'd be considered unattractive.

But when Jerome got out of his chair and took my hand, he guided me to stand so that he could hug me. That was the moment I knew that I had found an exceptional man with whom I was perfectly compatible. He whispered in my ear, "No one deserves this more than you."

"Thank you," I said.

We kissed right there by our table in the intimate restaurant. Out of the corner of my eye, I saw Giovanni coming toward us.

Jerome told him that I was promoted.

"Wow. Fantastic news. You'd better buy her a nice bottle of wine," Giovanni said.

"On me tonight," I said. "Finest you got. What do you recommend?"

Giovanni nodded. "For a festive occasion like this, it has to be Incisa della Rocchetta Sassicaia."

"Sounds good," I said. "Let's have a bottle of that."

Giovanni said we would love it and turned to get the wine. He whispered, "I can't let you pay."

"Why not? This is how I want to celebrate."

"Yeah, but…" He hesitated at first, but spoke with conviction, "Then why don't you let me celebrate you?"

"Because I just got a huge raise and I have money to burn."

"Save it. There might be something you want."

"I already know what I want. That's what I want to talk to you about."

"What is it?"

"Well, hold on. First you have to let me agree to pay for dinner."

"Not on your life."

"Why are you being so stubborn about this?" *Because if you're so stubborn about my not paying for dinner, how can you possibly be okay with the other stuff I want to talk about?*

"Because I have some news, too."

"Oh…" I said. *Well that makes sense, then.* "You first."

"It's not the kind of news that you just say. It'll come. Just wait."

"Oka-ay," I said, unsure of his meaning. *Why are you acting so weird, Jerome?*

"So, you first. What would you like to talk about?"

"Well," I began. I swallowed hard and gathered up my nerve. "You know how you want to leave Porter & Sons and launch your own business?"

"Eventually. After I save for the start-up and Aidan's education."

"Right," I said. "What if you had another investor?"

"What do you mean?"

*Gulp.* "I mean me."

He shook his head. "No, Monique. No. I could never take your money."

"You wouldn't be. It's not a gift. It'd be an investment."

"But what if it fails?"

"It won't. You were successful before, remember?" I added, "Besides, I've seen you in action at the community garden. You know what you're doing."

He got that look in his eyes again. They sparkled every time the new venture was on his mind. "I haven't told you this yet, but already now without the renovation I have planned, they want to do a segment on the garden on The Food Network. I got a call from one of the producers."

"Jerome, that's great!"

"Yeah, but the income and benefits I have right now…" He looked like he was at war with himself. "It doesn't seem like the right time yet. I need to do a huge overhaul of the space and that means permits and contractors and…"

"Capital," I added. "I can help. Not as a favor, but as part owner. Silent owner."

"Is this just because you got your promotion?"

"And a bonus."

"Well, what about your condo? Don't you want to pay it off?"

"I will. I am. There's plenty for both."

"There is?"

"Do you have any idea what size of check my bonus will be?"

He shook his head. "Actually, I don't."

I told him and his jaw actually dropped. He was shocked. "That's like six times the amount I got last year, and I thought I'd won the lottery."

I nodded. "Told you. There are new options now."

"I see." He seemed hesitant, like he'd come up to Cloud Nine with me, but then dropped to a lower cloud. His posture changed. I could tell that he was uncomfortable, because he pushed his chair back and sat up, his back stiff.

"Look," he said, "I was raised in a pretty traditional family. It's a lot to wrap my mind around the idea that my girlfriend makes that much more than me. It's going to take a minute for that to sink in."

"Should I not have told you my bonus amount? I want us to be able to talk about this stuff." *Come on, Jerome!*

He looked down at his plate. I sensed that he had left our conversation and retreated into his own world.

"Ugh" — he rested his forehead in his cupped hand — "I never wanted to turn into my dad. I never wanted to be like him."

"What's he like?"

"When I was around fifteen or so, my mom had a chance to get promoted. We're talking big promotion. Like, the family could have lived on easy street. The only catch was we'd have had to move. My dad wouldn't do it. He flat out refused. Came up with a million reasons why not, but the only real reason was pride."

"I see."

"And my mom is still bitter about it. Every time they can't afford to do something — say, take a trip or buy a new couch, they fight about it."

"That must be painful for you."

"It is. They fight a lot and I understand it. He stood in her way. But he couldn't handle the idea of her being the main breadwinner. You see, if we had moved, he wouldn't have had to work. The whole family could have lived on my mom's income."

I nodded, trying to show him that I was listening. I knew this was infinitely more complicated for him than it was for me. I had wanted to make him happy with the idea, not force him to face his demons.

"She almost left him over it. I understood her then and I still understand her. It would suck to have to give up something you really wanted, something you worked really hard for because of some jerk's male ego. I get it."

I was shocked to hear Jerome describe his dad that way.

"Maybe she was in love with the jerk?" I offered. "Maybe the jerk was a good father and good husband in other ways?"

"He was. He still is. You know, he has never once let her carry in the groceries. Even when his back was all messed up. He actually arranged for the neighbor's kid to come and carry in the groceries. He's that kind of man. But I guess that's what I'm saying. He's traditional. They both are, in a way."

"I feel strange that I haven't met them."

"We'll go at Christmas," Jerome said. His tone was matter-of-fact.

I was taken aback by his declaration. Had he decided on both of our behalves that we'd do that?

"Oh will we now? I was kind of thinking I'd like to introduce you to my mom."

"But I already told them we're coming."

"Why would you do that without talking to me about it first?"

"I don't know. I just assumed."

That irked me. "Never assume." I sounded curt, but I was mad. I hadn't lived this long by my own rules only to have my guy decide on things like where we spent our holiday.

"All right," he said. "I get it. I shouldn't have, but can we go see them? They're really looking forward to meeting you."

"What about my mom?"

"New Year's?"

"Nobody cares about New Year's. Christmas is the important holiday."

For some reason, I was fuming over this. It was silly, in a way, and I knew it. Mom didn't really care for the holiday at all, but it was the principle. Most years when I was growing up, I went to Claudia's since Mom was pagan. Then it hit me. "Oh my God. We're having our first fight," I said.

Jerome's face softened immediately. "Is that what this is? I was starting to get afraid that you were going to dump me."

"Dump you?"

"I thought maybe that was where this was going."

"No. I was mad. I am mad. I'll be mad until we come to an agreement about our holiday plans, but I wouldn't dump you just for that," I said. "But I do want you to check with me before you book up my time."

"I understand."

"And I'd be delighted to meet your parents at Christmas. Let's have Solstice with my mom. That's the big holiday for her."

"Solstice?"

"I have a hippie mom."

He smiled like he thought it was funny. "I see."

"She's pagan."

"Like a witch?"

"No. Like a pagan."

"Oh," he said. "We're Christians."

"Oh."

"Good Christians. The church-going kind," he added. It made me pause. I wasn't sure how to respond because I didn't know what he meant by it.

"Ah," I said vaguely, having never before considered the possibility that we might be on different pages where religion was concerned. "But you don't go to church, do you?"

"I do when I visit my family and, yeah, I sometimes go on my own."

"Oh." I sounded judgmental and I knew it. *Open your mind, Monique. This is Jerome, the guy you're in love with.* But I knew he could perceive my hesitation.

"What's wrong with that?"

"Nothing. But you don't expect me to go with you, do you?"

"Well, not yet…"

"What do you mean *not yet*?"

"Not right now."

"So, sometime in the future?" I asked. "When?"

"Well, I mean, if we were to…"

"What?"

"If we had kids, let's say…"

Giovanni returned with the wine and, from afar I could see that beside it there was a dark red velour-covered little box, the size of… *Holy shit!* An engagement ring.

Jerome's forehead was covered in tiny beads of sweat and my insides felt woozy. I thought I might throw up. This was the worst possible timing of all timing ever. This could not be more awkward. Could a first fight lead to a marriage proposal? Only in a movie starring Meg Ryan or someone like that. This was my life and it seemed, very suddenly, to be falling apart. *Why are you telling me how to raise our kids? Why are you trying to tie me down for life? How can I possibly get married to a guy who doesn't want me to be successful?*

"Excuse me," I said, and got up to go to the washroom. What a disaster this was.

"Where's she going?" Giovanni asked. "Did I get it wrong?"

"It's okay," I heard Jerome say from afar. "I'll take that."

I knew he meant the ring. I felt sick. In the safety of the stall, I let my tears come. Maybe he wasn't the perfect guy. I didn't want to give up my dreams for his. I didn't want to convert to his religion. I didn't want him to feel like less of a man because I made more than him. I didn't want him to pay for dinner. All I wanted was to end this nightmare. How had I not seen the signs? How had I fallen so hard, so fast?

I cried like the dream was over, like I'd awoken to find myself in the worst possible reality I could imagine. I didn't want to be with a backwards thinking alpha male. Maybe that's precisely why for my entire adult life I'd kept all men at arm's length. I'd kept my distance because clearly, when you let your guard down, men just try to take advantage. I could hear my mom's voice in my head—*'All men want to do is dominate and stand in the way of your dreams.'* I hadn't told Jerome why she was single and maybe I wouldn't now. Maybe I'd keep it to myself that my mom had made the choice that his mom couldn't. My mom had tossed out the guy who had stood in the way of her dreams. That was the difference between our two families. And the truth was, I was just like my mom. If I had to choose, I would take my freedom. I would take my career, my friends and my single-occupancy home. I would have everything my way, if it came down to choosing between a man and all that.

I was in full-on sob mode when a woman came into the washroom. She knocked on my stall. There were two in here. I thought it was rude of her.

"Can't you use the other one?" I asked.

"I want to talk with you."

"Who are you?"

"I'm Maria, Giovanni's wife. He called me and said he just ruined your life and I need to come save you, so open up. I was watching *Law and Order SVU* and I want to get back to it."

I opened the stall. I didn't dare not to, with an introduction like that. This woman meant business.

"Yes?"

"Dry your eyes."

I took some toilet paper and patted my tears. So far, it felt like Maria could make me do anything.

"Okay, so tell me. Why don't you want to marry that handsome man out there? Giovanni says he's a nice guy." She pulled up the wooden chair that was in the restroom off to the side, as though decades ago they had had no storage space and someone had tossed it in here.

But when she sat on it and faced me, I wondered if other women had had breakdowns in here before. Maria looked comfortable.

I had nothing to lose. I needed to let it out. "I think I might have made a terrible mistake in getting together with him."

"Do you love him?"

I shuddered at the thought that I had unwittingly fallen in love with a guy who wanted to convert me and keep me at a lower earning potential than him. I scoffed and said, "Yeah." But quickly added, "I can get over him, though."

When I spoke the words aloud, I realized that I probably wouldn't get over it. So I put my face in my lap and tried my best to enclose myself inside the shelter my arms provided. "No," I sobbed. "I'll never get over him."

"You know, it takes a long time to teach a man what you're like and how you want to be treated. Do you have any idea how long Giovanni took to understand that when I'm watching SVU, I'm not available? Look! He still doesn't understand." She laughed. "That's what men are like. If you love them, you find a way to teach them."

"But that's the thing. Up until about fifteen minutes ago, I thought I wouldn't have to teach him anything. But now I just found out he doesn't like that I make more than him and he wants to raise our kids in the church."

"Nothing wrong with raising kids with a good moral foundation," she said.

"I know," I protested. "I just... He never told me he went to church and he wants us to go see his parents for Christmas."

"Because he's proud of you. He wants them to meet the woman he loves. What's wrong with that?"

Maria wasn't having any of my protestations. It felt hopeless. "We've only been dating for a few months. It's too soon for him to ask me to marry him."

"Let him ask. Doesn't mean you have to say yes and it doesn't mean it's gotta happen this year."

"It's so not happening this year. There's just no way."

"But you want it to happen?"

"Of course I do. He's my soulmate."

"There you go." She clapped her hands together looking satisfied with herself. "That's what you have to tell him. That's all. And take a peek at the ring. If you like it, you can wear it. What's the harm?"

"But there's so much I don't know about him."

"That is the whole point of marriage, honey." She got up and gestured for me to do the same. She hugged me and said, "If you knew everything, married life would be very boring."

"Thank you, Maria."

"Don't thank me. Thank Giovanni. He's going to be giving me one hour of feet rubbing later for this. That's marriage."

\* \* \* \*

When I returned to the table, Jerome got up. His face was sullen. I felt like I had single-handedly ripped his heart out and stomped on it.

"I'm sorry," he said.

"No, I am." I hugged him. "I love you, Jerome. And I think you might be my soulmate, but I have been alone for a very long time and the idea that we found each other is going to take some getting used to."

"So you're not saying no?"

"I'm saying I think we should wait."

"Baby, I can wait as long as you want. I will ask you again and again. As many times as you can handle. If I think that someday you're going to say yes, I'm just going to keep on asking."

"I'd like that."

He grabbed me and kissed me. Giovanni and Maria stood off to the side. I saw from the corner of my eye that Giovanni put his arms around Maria and pulled her in close, whispered something in her ear then kissed her cheek. She transformed completely and became a blushing shy girl. I understood what she had told me. She was an angel to me. And I knew right there and then that I wanted exactly what they had—a solid understanding of each other, a tenderness that had not been broken even after years of being together. I wanted Jerome. I just didn't want to be married yet.

We sat down again.

"We should finish this wine," Jerome said. "And celebrate you moving up in the world."

"Can I see the ring?"

"But…"

"Please?"

He took it out of his shirt pocket and handed me the tiny dark red box. I opened it and, inside, there was a gleaming sparkling diamond on a white gold band. It was simple and elegant and precisely what I would have chosen if I'd gone shopping for myself.

"It's beautiful," I heard myself say, though I felt like I was in a daze.

"I'm glad you like it. You know, we could call it something else."

"Like a promise ring?"

"Exactly." He nodded. "What do you think?"

"I think that's the sweetest thing ever."

"Monique Mackenzie, I promise to keep asking you to marry me until you are ready to say yes." He took my hand and put the ring on my ring finger. It sparkled in the candlelight and I couldn't help but gasp in awe.

"Jerome Fontaine, I promise you that one day I will say yes."

We kissed again, this time across the table. It was awkward because we both stood and we couldn't concentrate on kissing because there was a candle on the table and I felt the heat against my top. But this time the whole restaurant cheered. I hadn't noticed that they'd all stopped eating and had been paying attention to us for the past few minutes. Somehow everything around us had ceased to matter and all I could see was Jerome. The applause and the acknowledgment that this was a special once-in-a-lifetime moment was so welcome. And the most wonderful part of all was that Maria gave me a nod of approval right before she turned and walked out onto the patio and up the back steps to their suite upstairs.

"I can't believe that when I introduce you to my mom, I'll be wearing this." I shook my head in disbelief. "I've never so much as introduced her to any guy before."

"Never?"

I shook my head. "Never."

"I'm honored," he said. "I'll do my best to make a good impression."

"Awesome," I said. "So you'll howl to the moon and dance in a circle with us?"

"Is that seriously how you celebrate the Solstice?"

I smiled. I tried my best to fool him, but I couldn't pull it off. "No, silly. We'll light some candles and have some nice food and that'll be that."

"Sounds easy enough. I can handle that."

"And I've been to church plenty of times, just so you know. Claudia's family goes every year, too, so I tagged along. But I've also been on other occasions."

"Oh yeah?"

"Sure. There was a really progressive one right across the street from me in my old place and they had this wonderful mystical labyrinth in the rectory. I used to walk it quite regularly. They played music on Friday nights. It was very cool."

"I love you," Jerome said. This time his voice had that classic tone of full conviction that he was so good at.

And I hung on his every word. I knew beyond anything I'd ever known in my life that this man was my soul mate.

"I love you, too," I said. "So, what do you think of my investment proposal?"

"Well, I think it's very generous of you, but I don't need it. I wanted to tell you some major news, and clearly I should have said something before."

"What is it?"

"I got a really sweet offer from the city. They want to give me the permits and the licenses I need. The mayor wants us to be a leading pioneer in community garden development. And I got a call from Thomas Quinn, the chef at Sheraton, that he wants first dibs on developing a menu."

"So it's all happening?"

He beamed from ear to ear. "It's all happening, baby. And I want you to be a part of the excitement. I want you with me every step of the way. But I don't want your money. This is my project. My other baby. So I guess you'll just have to spend a little more time at the spa. Or, hell, buy a spa."

I laughed. I was so happy for him and actually a little relieved to not be completely enmeshed. I saw the wisdom in his choice. And how cool that I was soon to be engaged to the city's next big thing. I could already see him on the cover of local business magazines talking about sustainable practices, giving of his heart and passion to the community that he loved. His generosity was such a turn-on.

"Take me home, Jerome. I want to show you what this ring does to me."

"Mmm, baby. You got it."

* * * *

At my place, I wasted no time. I had him stripped down in mere seconds of walking in the door. I wanted to climb on top of him and show him just how wet he made me, but he slowed me down. I was already so desperate for him — from everything we'd been through that evening — that I wanted to get to the main course, but just like in regular life, Jerome had his own plan and something told me it was a good one.

"Baby, let me massage you," he insisted. He lit candles, including a special one that turned into hot oil as it melted in its metal container. He undressed me slowly and tossed me down onto the bed, rubbing my back and shoulders the way he knew I liked. He kneaded the tension away, and I gave in completely.

I was more than just a little wet by the time he fingered my pussy. He turned me on my back and had me. His cock inside me, I wrapped my legs around him to show him how badly I wanted him. His weight on me was a real turn-on and the angle of his thrusting was perfect. We found our rhythm and I yelped out when my orgasm came. He slowed down his pace, which extended my climax for what seemed like a really long time. In that sublime state, I had a moment of pure clarity, and knew wholeheartedly that I wanted to be married to him forever.

He finished inside me, letting out a moan and steadying himself as he held me.

"Jerome," I said. "Ask me again."

His voice was quiet, humble. He was still inside me. "Will you marry me?"

"Yes," I said, tangled in the sheets with the man I loved.

* * * *

"Claudia," I panted into the phone after running all the way through the mall to get to the drug store before it closed. "I need you to come over."

"Now? Why? What's the matter?" She sounded worried. She could read me better than anyone.

"I can't explain. Just come."

"All right," she said and with that, I went back to rushing.

I paid for my purchase at the drug store then ran down to the subway station and managed to hop through the door fast enough to get onto the first train headed home. Once I was out the doors again, I ran up the stairs, not bothering to take the escalator. I was filled with energy and had no idea how to get it out of my system. By the time I was through my front door, I was drained with sweat.

Claudia arrived five minutes after I did. I had only just taken off my boots and stripped out of my work clothes. Today called for flannel pajamas and fluffy pink bunny slippers. I opened the door for Claudia and she hugged me immediately. "What's up?" she asked.

"Uh," I said, hurrying her inside. Once the door was closed, I said, "I'm late."

"You mean?"

"I've been on schedule for my entire adult life, ever since I started bleeding."

"Are you on the pill?"

"Of course I am!"

"And you've never been late before?"

"Never."

It was impossible to keep up with the myriad thoughts that flooded my brain. Scenarios played themselves out for me like my life was a collection of potential movies. Some were comedies and romances but others were horror films. I was flooded with emotions and didn't know what to think. "You have to be here. I can't do this alone."

"I'm here," Claudia said. "I'm always here for you. No matter what happens, okay?"

I nodded. She put her arms around me. And patted the back of my head like I was her child and needed reassurance. It was exactly what I needed to feel. As much as I wanted to involve Jerome in this process, some things were meant for best friends and best friends only.

"Have you guys been using condoms, too?" Claudia asked. And in a way that only a best friend can, she teased me and said, "Or has Fort Knox decided to open some windows?"

"Well, uh—" It was so hard to admit. "I relaxed a bit on my rules."

"Do you think maybe somewhere deep inside that very stylish exterior of yours, you might actually want to be a mother?"

The tears flooded. She got it completely. She got me. She knew the precise thought that had been plaguing me so deep inside my own psyche that I couldn't even recognize it. I nodded. "Claudia, I've changed."

"You met your soulmate," she said gently. "That changes things."

"But I was one hundred percent career woman—and sassy lady about town. I was Samantha!"

"You can still be Samantha."

"No, I can't. I don't think I am anymore."

"It's okay, Monique. People change."

I nestled into her neck and let myself sob it out. I needed the tears to flow and I knew she would catch them, like she always had. She was my guardian angel and always had been.

"I don't know what to tell Jerome. He thinks I don't want kids."

"First of all, don't worry about Jerome. This is about you and your body and your future. You need to make your own decisions. But second, doesn't he want kids?"

"He said he did but that he was perfectly happy to just have Aidan, too."

"And you? What do you think? Where do you see yourself?"

"I'm ambitious. You know that."

"Oh, I do."

She nodded as she patted my back. We moved over to the couch and sat down.

"But Jerome wants to work from home. He wants out of the whole corporate rat race. He never wanted in to begin with, actually."

"So he could be a hot stay-at-home dad, maybe?"

I nodded. "Something like that."

"That's a pretty cool set-up. And very you. Samantha would approve."

"We haven't talked about it yet."

"You haven't even done the test yet."

"You're right. It's over there." I pointed to my handbag, tossed randomly to the floor near the front door.

"Do you feel ready?"

"I feel nervous."

"I'm here."

She got up and went over to my purse. Rummaging through it, she took out the white paper bag I'd bought at the drug store. She motioned to me to come with her as she headed for the bathroom.

"It's time," she said.

As I caught up with her she handed me the white package like she was passing me a baton. I took hold of the handful that could potentially take my life in a completely new direction.

"So I just pee on it?"

"You've never done one before?"

"No. I'm Fort Knox, remember?"

"Seriously? Never?"

"I may have been pretty adventurous in my day, but I was really, really careful."

"All right. Well, yeah, you just pee on it."

I took it from the package and pulled my flannel jammies down then squatted over the toilet. No matter how hard I concentrated, I couldn't get myself to do it.

We were silent for well over a minute before Claudia said, "You could also pee into a cup."

"That sounds easier. Can you get one?"

"For sure," she said, leaving the bathroom. "Which one do you want to use?" she called from the kitchen.

"Doesn't matter."

"Okay." She came back with a mug shaped like Mickey Mouse.

"Not that one. My mom got me that at Disneyland when I was twelve."

"Really?" She looked surprised. "Why didn't I know that?"

I shrugged.

"How about a mason jar?"

"Okay."

She came back with one. Mostly likely, she had found it on the dish rack, meaning that it was the one I had used yesterday to bring my mid-morning snack of frozen fruit and yogurt to work with me. How strange that it would now play this much larger role in my destiny? Claudia passed it to me. I held it beneath myself. I was in the most awkward position imaginable.

"Is that a ring?" Claudia asked. "Oh my God! You're engaged?"

"Yes. I meant to tell you. I really did. But then this whole thing happened and…"

"Tell me now," she said.

"I can't. I need to concentrate."

"Okay, okay, just think about waterfalls." She propped herself up on the counter and watched, which didn't make it better but I didn't want her to leave. I couldn't handle being alone right now. I needed her.

When I'd finished, Claudia took the mason jar from me and set it on the counter and popped the white stick into it.

"Now we wait," she said.

"How long?"

"Not long. Pull up your pants and wash your hands."

"Seriously?"

"Welcome to the future, modern woman."

She knew just how to handle me in this awkward mess. How horribly I would have managed if I hadn't had her. But I did have her. I had the best friend in the entire world.

"Claudia," I said after I wiped my hands on the towel. "Thank you for being here."

"Always," she said. She hugged me. "Are you ready to look?"

"You look."

"Okay," she said, picking the stick out of the jar and taking a glance at it. "Blue line means baby. No line means no baby. Let me ask you one more time. In your heart of hearts, what do you want this stick to say?"

My pulse raced. It seemed to tear me apart inside. "I can't say it. I can't say it."

"Yes, Monique, you can."

"Okay," I said. "Blue line."

She hugged me so tight I thought she was going to squeeze my ribcage to the breaking point. "You're going to be a great mother," she said. "But not yet."

"There's no line?"

"No line." She held it up for me to see and sure enough, it was just white. "They're not totally accurate all the time, so you might want to check with your doctor but…"

"No line." I nodded. I felt a wave of relief come over me. "Good," I said. "I wasn't ready for everything to change so quickly."

"No, but you are ready for change."

"I am. I know that now."

I could safely tell Jerome about this experience and I knew that he would be delighted to hear the conclusion I'd come to. I was delighted. Who would have thought that in my deepest heart I wanted something that I hadn't even known I wanted?

"How do you feel?" Claudia asked.

"Like I want a glass of pinot grigio."

"I could go for one, too."

"Let's do it."

There were many scenarios to play with now and they didn't seem as scary or as far away as they once had. I believed in Jerome's business. I believed in my own career. But there was no rush for us to start our family. We could take it slow, live together, talk about marriage. There was time for all of that. But I knew now that I wanted something much larger than any of the stuff I used to care about. I wanted a family. My own family.

I had the beginnings of one already. Here I was toasting the universe with my best friend in the entire world, a woman I loved more than anyone. And later, I would see Jerome and tell him about all of this and I knew that he would look at me with awe and wonder. I knew that he would accept everything about me. I knew that I had found my soulmate and that his family would become my own. I thought about Aidan, about how we might tell him when the time came that he was going to have a little brother or sister.

"Claudia," I said. "I love you."

"Aww, honey." She hugged me. "I love you right back."

She took me by the hand and lifted it up so she could get a closer look at the ring. "Beautiful," she said. "Tell me everything."

# About the Author

Romance heroines have saved my sanity numerous times through break-ups and life changes. I find escaping into a romance both soothing and revitalizing—and even better when there are some steamy scenes to tantalize the imagination.

For most of my adult life, I've concentrated on carving out a serious career, but a number of love-hungry, sassy characters keep taking over my mind, insisting that I daydream, live vicariously through them and tell their stories. Watching these women emerge on the page gives me a different sort of satisfaction than I get from my day job. It is a joy to share them with readers.

I live in a tiny apartment in a crowded city and I like to think there is something romantic about this. I did manage to find my soul mate here.

Destiny Moon loves to hear from readers. You can find her contact information, website details and author profile page at http://www.totallybound.com.

Totally Bound Publishing